A GOOD MARINE

A Novel
by
Tracey L. Thompson

ISBN: 9798638492441

DEDICATION

This book is dedicated to my brother-in-law, Gregory Payran Thompson, who committed suicide in March of 2014. Greg was a corrections officer at a California State Prison. Shortly after Greg's suicide, this story came to me mixed in with the experiences my son, Leverto Olmedo, had in the U.S. Marine Corps and the experiences my brother, William Edward Savage, had in Army boot camp.

So valuable to heaven is the dignity of the human soul that every member of the human race has a guardian angel from the moment the person begins to be.

—St. Jerome

CONTENTS

AUTHOR'S NOTE

Who is Aevery Warrier?

Simply put, he's Every Warrior. Every Marine, everyone who's served in an army, everyone who's fought an enemy. Everyone who needs to meet his or her guardian angel.

The concepts in this story could apply to every warrior that sees combat, and those who don't; I want readers to see that this book could be about anyone in the military. His last name is Warrier because he could be any warrior, of any branch of the military. So, Every Warrior became Aevery Warrier. I use his first name from the beginning because he is Aevery throughout the entire story. His drill instructor refers to him as "Recruit Warrier," but we as the audience see him as Aevery. All of his buddies are referred to by their last names because that is how they refer to each other.

The Isle of Apples, Shining Isle and Sunless Sea come from *The Pagan Book of Living and Dying* by Starhawk and M. Macha Nightmare. I hope everyone who reads this book will also understand concepts related to the spirit world, like the Rainbow Bridge (Native American and Norse mythology). The Rainbow Bridge can also be found in the book *The Thirteen Original Clan Mothers* by Jaime Sams.

Foreword

Military service is not easy on a family, and very few spouses can put up with the constant training, deployments, outbursts, apologies, anger management problems, and—for many—drinking problems.

This will not be over quickly.
You will not enjoy this.
—Spoken by the Queen of Sparta in
the movie *300*

That's how I would describe a deployment. You are away from your family, friends and all the comforts that normal Americans take for granted every single day.

My mother, Tracey L. Thompson, was there for me through my deployments. I would usually call her once a week and she was sure to get a list of things that I wanted for my next care package. Jerky, licorice, and trail mix were usually my top three choices. Even if the care packages always showed up with embarrassing things drawn all over them like "my schmoopsie," they were still the highlight of my day. Having someone to vent to and listen to your complaints is a strong plus on those long months away from home.

Even for those with a fantastic support structure in place, many active duty military and veterans find it hard to cope with the psychological effects not just from service, but also from the stress service puts on relationships with family members.

A ramp ceremony is a memorial service for a fallen comrade. It is held either at the airport prior to the departure of the aircraft carrying the deceased person's body or at the arrival of the same aircraft at the deceased's home base. If you live, you may get to attend it. If your unit is still in active combat, you probably will not even get to say goodbye. Some personnel were not even old enough to consume alcohol in the country that they died to protect. These are some of the things that I think of when a random bystander thanks me for my service. The pain and struggles that they will never have to endure. I pity them and sometimes envy their ignorance.

According to data from the Department of Veterans Affairs, as of 2016 roughly 6,000 veterans kill themselves every year. That's an average of sixteen per day. That number is just a statistic to most people, but there are faces that come to my mind when I read it. I have personally known some of those men.

Life is certainly worth living. There is nothing wrong with getting help. Resilience is the capacity to recover quickly from difficulties. It's toughness.

Getting through difficult times is what strengthens your resilience.

> Suicide doesn't end the chances
> of life getting worse; it eliminates
> the possibility of it ever getting any
> better.
> —Unknown

Leverto Olmedo
United States Marine Corps Veteran, Sergeant of Marines
Operation Iraqi Freedom Veteran
Operation Enduring Freedom Veteran
Master Instructor Suicide Prevention Trainer
Eldest son of Tracey L. Thompson

Preface

I come from a military family. My great-grandfather served in the Army in World War I, my grandfather served in the Army in World War II, my uncle served in the Korean War and was a POW, my father served in the Navy as a Seabee in Vietnam, my brother served in the National Guard, and my son served nine years in the US Marine Corps and was deployed to Iraq and Afghanistan. I worked as a barber for Marine Corps Community Services, and years later worked for the FOCUS Project helping to teach resiliency skills to Marine Corps families.

I have seen what PTSD did to my father and what it has done to my son. Four years ago, my brother-in-law, who was a prison guard, committed suicide. I wondered if he regretted his decision.

This story was inspired by all of these experiences. What would happen if a suicidal Marine could see the consequences of his suicide before he decided on that permanent solution? *A Good Marine* is that story.

A GOOD MARINE

Prologue

The year was 1991 at the U.S. Marine Corps Recruit Depot, San Diego. The mustard yellow buildings had seen a myriad of recruits become Marines. Nineteen-year-old Aevery Warrier stood in a large warehouse with a group of recruits in the supply line. His head had just been shaved, and he had been given a sea bag. All the recruits quickly got their supplies.

"What size?" the supply worker shouted at Aevery.

"Twelve, ma'am!" he shouted back.

She got a pair of boots and set them out on the front of the table. Aevery stuffed them into his sea bag and moved to the next station.

Eighteen-year-old Russell Larson moved up behind Aevery.

"What size?"

"Ten, ma'am!" Recruit Larson grabbed his boots and stuffed them into his sea bag.

All the recruits were in a school circle around twenty-three-year-old Drill Instructor (DI) Sergeant Fram, who had a thick southern accent.

"When I say 'left,' you don't move," he instructed, "That is the preparatory command. When I say 'face,' that's when you all move together. And *make sure you flare your fucking heels!*" He demonstrated as he talked and emphasized the flare.

Out on the Parade Deck, DI Fram called drill. It was still early in their training; the recruits were still not blousing their boots. A second Drill Instructor, thirty-one-year-old Staff Sergeant Sanchez, ran around the recruits and checked for mistakes, making small corrections when needed.

Then DI Sanchez gave a hand signal to DI Fram to halt the platoon, and he called the platoon to a halt. The whole platoon stood at attention. DI Sanchez called DI Fram to come to the back of the platoon. The drill instructors were standing there, towering over the turd. They were talking to each other under their breath.

Finally, DI Sanchez shouted at the platoon, "School circle around me right now!"

All the recruits ran as fast as they could to school circle, almost falling over when they slammed to a stop.

"Eyeballs on my turd!" DI Sanchez shouted.

"Click, sir!" the recruits shouted in unison. All eyes were indeed on the turd, and all the recruits were scared.

DI Sanchez was abnormally calm. "Who *the fuck*—shit their pants?"

Dead silence.

An evil grin washed over DI Sanchez' face, "Good. Form it up right now!"

The recruits ran to formation, looks of dread on their faces.

Eighteen-year-old recruit Higgins lagged behind. After everyone had already moved, he made his decision. "Sir," he said, "this recruit did, Sir!" He sounded like he was expecting some sort of mercy for speaking up.

But DI Sanchez never showed any mercy. "Good. Higgins, put that fucking turd in your pocket and get the fuck back into formation." He raised his voice now, shouting at the whole platoon, "It's too late—*you're all fucked*. As far as I'm concerned, *every* recruit just shit on my parade deck. *You're all gonna fucking die!*"

Higgins ran over to the turd, stuffed it in his cargo pocket, wiped his hand on his pants, and got back in formation.

Nineteen-year-old recruit Smith whispered to Higgins, "Wait till we get back, bitch. You have to sleep sometime."

Later that afternoon, the smell of shit permeated the Squad Bay, as all the recruits were struggling to do pushups, their blouses were drenched with sweat. Higgins lay on the floor, whimpering. The turd had now become a permanent part of his cargo pocket.

DI Sanchez was still angry. "On my fucking parade deck!" he bellowed.

DI Fram stood over Higgins as he tried to push up and fell back down, still whimpering. "This recruit can't do any more," he said to DI Sanchez.

"Recruit Higgins," DI Sanchez said, "sit up and

take a break." He looked at the others. "Your fellow recruits will do yours for you."

Higgins, not realizing the kind of animosity he was provoking, sat on his footlocker, while all the others did pushups.

Aevery, sweat dripping from his nose and chin, shot an angry look at recruit Larson.

That evening at sunset, four recruits (Higgins, Fire Team Leader Aevery, Squad Leader Larson, and another recruit they called The Guide), scrubbed the parade deck on their hands and knees using a large pail of soapy water and a scuzz brush. A huge area around them was wet and soapy.

That night, as all the recruits lay at attention on their neatly made racks, DI Fram, who was standing at the front of the Squad Bay, shouted, "Adjust!" Recruits slapped their beds twice, clapped their hands twice, and snapped their fingers twice.

"Hit the lights!" DI Fram shouted.

The Fire Watch recruit hit the lights.

DI Fram took off his cover (or "Smokey the Bear hat," as it is affectionately called) and retired to the duty hut.

A while later, Higgins smacked the huge wooden door knocker on the side of the Drill Instructors' door, which woke up several of the recruits, including Aevery. *This dumb mutherfucker,* Aevery thought. *What shit is he gonna stir up now?*

"This recruit requests permission to speak to

Drill Instructor, Sergeant Fram," Higgins yelled at the door.

"Higgins," the DI shouted back, "What the fuck do you want?" His voice was muffled by the closed door. "Why aren't you fucking sleeping?" The DI's reaction filled Aevery with relief and joy.

"This recruit's bed is wet with soapy water," Higgins called through the door.

Oh, fuck! Aevery thought. He imagined a scenario where they would be scrubbing floors and making beds over and over for the rest of the night. He also listened intently for the drill instructor's next response.

The drill instructor threw the door open. "Why are you telling me? I don't give a shit!" He was dressed in physical training gear, his olive drab undershirt tucked neatly into his shiny, olive drab, athletic shorts, plus flip flops and his DI cover mounted impeccably on his head. "Get the fuck back to your rack," he pointed at the bed, "and don't bother me again or you'll be on fire watch until you die!" He slammed the door in Higgins' face.

Aevery lay there in the dark, a smirk of satisfaction on his face. He didn't know who had thrown soapy water on Higgins' rack, but he sure wanted to shake that ballsy recruit's hand.

Weeks later, the recruits were on the obstacle course. Aevery looked down the steep wall he was supposed to rappel. He was trying to get up enough nerve to jump.

Just then, DI Fram appeared behind him, hanging upside down, "What the fuck is taking you so long, Recruit Warrier?" he shouted. "Get it movin'!"

Aevery jumped and immediately rappelled down the wall.

Days turned into weeks, weeks into months. Aevery thought his graduation day would never come. But the day finally arrived when Aevery and the rest of his platoon were all standing at attention on the Parade Deck and trying not to look out at the bleachers packed with families and friends. When his turn came, he received his Eagle, Globe & Anchor. He was now a Marine. Not merely a lowly recruit anymore, but a Marine. He fantasized that his mother and his nana were watching and saw every moment as he marched in with his platoon. He daydreamed about how they would come and congratulate him after the ceremony and how he would tell them all his heart-wrenching and funny stories about boot camp. He couldn't wait to see them. He even looked forward to seeing his little brother, Tony. He had written several letters to his family during boot camp, but he'd never gotten a response.

After the graduation ceremony, while all the recruits from Aevery's platoon were visiting with their parents and families, Aevery looked around hopefully. No one from his family was there. He looked and looked, but everywhere he turned, he saw nothing but strangers.

Fast forward two years to 1993, which found Aevery serving at the Forward Operating Base (FOB) in Mogadishu.

All the Marines were gathered for mail call. The mail rep handed out packages. Only a few, including Aevery, received nothing. Aevery walked away feeling sad.

Later that day, all the Marines sat on their racks and enjoyed the contents of their packages. Aevery, who was now a Lance Corporal, looked on quietly. Even though he never got a package, he enjoyed seeing what the others received. He enjoyed their reaction to the items from home.

Larson, also now a Lance Corporal, turned to Aevery. "Warrier, you didn't get nothin' from home?" he asked through a mouthful of beef jerky. "Man, that's a tough break. Want some jerky?" He offered Aevery the bag, and he took a piece. Then Larson pulled out a plastic container. "My mom made these cookies. They're the best. Want one?"

Aevery greatly appreciated Larson's kindness. "Thanks, man."

"Just one. That's all you can have." Aevery took just one cookie. Larson smiled, and offered him a Twizzler. He pulled out a colorful box. "Oh, man!

Good & Plenty. My favorite candy!"

A minute later, Lance Corporal Johannas pulled a can out of his box. "Copenhagen Long Cut!"

"Hey!" Larson begged. Lemme get a pinch!" Johannas handed him the can.

Four years later, in 1997, several Marines gathered outside an office aboard the Quantico Marine Base in Virginia, for Aevery's promotion ceremony, where he pinned on Sergeant. Aevery's Commanding Officer and Senior Enlisted Advisor pinned him on. Larson and Johannas, now Corporals, congratulated him.

October 12th, 2000 found Aevery aboard a P-3 Orion flying over the Port of Aden in Yemen. As he and eleven other Marines flew over the USS *Cole,* smoke was still billowing out of the ship. Aevery was in full combat gear, his rifle between his legs. He looked out an observation window.

"Jesus Christ! Look at that mess! Sons-of-bitches." He shook his head.

Chapter One

Triggered

It had been three years since Gunnery Sergeant Aevery Warrier retired from the U.S. Marine Corps. This could have been like any other drunken night, but it wasn't. This particular night would go down as one of the most important nights of his life. If he survived.

He was sitting in his own bathtub, a bottle of bourbon in one hand, a 1911 pearl-handled revolver in the other. There was a bottle of prescription pain pills on the side of the tub. He took a swig of the bourbon and cleared his throat. As he sank deeper into the warm bath water and his drunken stupor, he drifted off into a nightmare that he knew all too well:

Floating in a skiff on a sea of blood, Aevery reached down and touched the water. He was horrified to see his bloody hand and looked frantically around the skiff. He noticed a piece of car wreckage floating in the distance. As it came closer, he saw the unconscious Marine on it, one leg missing from his charred body. Smoke rising from the bloody water began to cloud Aevery's vision. He squinted to see more clearly. Just then, dead Marine bodies began rising to the surface, suddenly surrounding him.

Startled awake Aevery sat bolt upright. He saw that he was still holding the pistol. His heavy breathing cut through the silence and echoed off the bathroom walls. To calm himself, he took another swig of bourbon and cleared his throat as the booze burned all the way down. But it didn't stop the memory of Corporal Larson from haunting his thoughts again. He remembered the night he'd been ordered to send a group on patrol in Iraq. All the men with him, he had hand-picked for the deployment. He knew them all. All were his brothers. His stomach turned over as the memory hit him and he saw his buddy, bloody and dead, being tucked into a body bag. He remembered almost peeing himself as the corpsman zipped the bag over Larson's face. He fought back tears now as he remembered loading his buddy onto the plane that would take his body home to his family.

The cold water jilted him out of the memory.

"Larson, you lucky son-of-a-bitch," he said aloud into the air, "it's all over for you, your suffering's done." He took another swig and cleared his throat again. "You lucky fucking bastard!" He looked at the pistol. "I wish I had the balls—"

Just then Aevery's devoted wife Candace, knocked at the door. "Are you all right in there? You've been in there for *hours!*" She tried the door, but it was locked. "Goddammit, Aevery, why do you have to lock the door?"

"For Christ sakes, Candace," he yelled at her. "I told you I just want to be left alone!" Still holding the pistol in one hand, he wrestled with the bottle. He shook two pills out, swigged them down, and cleared his throat. Then he checked the ammunition in the pistol.

Grumbling under her breath, Candace gave up and went downstairs.

Edward, a handsome, glowing spirit who looked to be a man in his forties, stood nearby. He was dressed in a USMC World War I Dress Blue Delta uniform. Aevery couldn't see him, but he was there. What Aevery was able to see was a beam of light streaking down into the bathroom. He didn't see it as it hit Edward, who was listening to something like he was on a phone call.

"Yeah, I think he's getting ready to do it," Edward said into the ethers. He paused and listened again. "Are you sure you want me to leave him here like this?" He listened again. "Okay, I'll be right there." Then he disappeared.

When Edward reappeared, he was standing in a huge heavenly courtroom. The floor was made of clouds, the ceiling was the night sky. He was standing before the Karmic Council of Seven Spiritual Beings, one of whom was Magda, who, although she looked to be in her sixties, had been alive for thousands of years. Her long silver hair was draped over the shoulders of her shimmering robes. She rose to her feet and faced Edward, her amethyst eyes filled with concern.

"You summoned me?" Edward asked.

"Because of where we are in Earth's history," she told him, "we have been given more leeway when it comes to intervening with suicides. We're going to allow you to intervene."

"Why now?"

Magda raised an eyebrow, "Because many human warriors are not fulfilling their Divine Purpose."

"Well," Edward said, "it looks like Gunnery Sergeant Aevery Warrier will be the next—"

Magda raised her voice, interrupting him, "—help him! Teach him a lesson!"

Edward looked at her. He was already feeling a little exasperated. "Pardon me, Your Honor, but you didn't allow me to intervene last time. How do I—?"

"—we *are* allowing it this time," she interrupted again.

"Yes, Your Honor," Edward acquiesced, lowering his head, but still looking at her.

"If he is allowed to continue on this path," she explained, "it will become his Karmic Loop. The Loop must be broken, Edward." As all Seven Spirits stood in unison, Magda continued, "You have been afforded this opportunity. Now go and do what you will, as long as it harm none. And as long as his free will remains intact. *Save him!*"

"I just hope I'm not too late." With that, Edward disappeared.

The wall along the staircase of the family home was decorated with framed photographs of Aevery and Candace's family. At the top of the stairs hung an older picture of a handsome man in Navy dress whites standing with his wife and teenage daughter. A bit lower were photos of a young man in a tuxedo with his date on prom night. Next was a four-year-old girl blowing out candles on her birthday cake with a smiling Aevery standing behind her. Near photos of Aevery and Candace on their wedding day hung photos from various deployment reunions with the family.

Candace had stuck with Aevery through nineteen years of marriage and raising two children as a Marine Corps wife through four deployments and six permanent changes of duty station. But for the past three years since his retirement, things had been going downhill fast. Candace was sound asleep on the sofa, above which hung a shadowbox filled with her husband's medals, award citations, and last promotion portrait, when a gunshot startled her awake.

Up in the bathroom, Aevery had just shot himself in the head. He was naked and dead and still in the bathtub. The wall behind him was covered with blood and brains. His eyes stared vacantly; his mouth was open and bloody. The gun was still in his dead hand. His spirit, dressed in USMC Dress Blue Deltas, with the rank of Gunnery Sergeant, stepped away from his body.

"Whoa...*what the fuck*?" Aevery was surprised to see his body.

Edward was standing behind him. "You feel better now?"

Aevery turned to look at Edward. "Yeah, actually, I do. Who are you?"

Edward gave him a friendly look. "I've been here with you the whole time. Hoping you wouldn't do it, but waiting to receive you, nonetheless. I'm Edward, your Guardian Angel."

"My Guardian Angel? Well, you certainly didn't do a very good job of guarding me." Aevery pointed to his own dead body. "Look what I just did."

"Ahhh, yes, the blame game. We're not allowed to tamper with your free will. Trust me, after this is all over with—" Edward gestured at the dead body "—we're going to have a nice, *long* conversation about everything." He gave a warm smile. There was even a twinkle in his eyes.

At the same time, Candace unlocked and opened the door. Horrified at the sight of her dead husband, she backed slowly out the door. Aevery followed her as she stumbled into the bedroom, reached for the bed, and stumbled again. She screamed and scrambled to get up, then ran out of the room.

He followed her into the hallway. "Wait! Candace—I didn't mean for you to find me like that. Wait!" But she could neither see him nor hear him.

Just then, Becka, their chubby seventeen-year-old daughter, came out of her bedroom tying her robe. She looked sleepy but shaken. "Mom? What was that shot I heard?"

"Get down the stairs!" Candace screamed. "Now!"

Becka blinked, looked around, and started to cry. Then she ran down the stairs, her mother right behind her. Aevery followed them to the living room and watched his widow dial the phone.

After a moment, she cried, "Please help me! My husband shot himself—I just found him!"

Becka began wailing. "Dad? No!" She tried to run for the stairs, but her mother grabbed her by the arm with one hand. "Come back here! You are NOT going up there!" She kept hold of Becka as she shouted into the phone, "Please come quickly!" Dropping the phone, she pushed Becka to the sofa and forced her to sit. "You sit right there. You are not going anywhere!" Taking a deep breath, she plopped down next to Becka and wiped her face on the sleeve of her pajamas.

Edward was standing nearby. Aevery was right in front of his family. "Candace," he said, "I'm sorry you were the one to find me. Look—I just couldn't take it anymore. I'm out of pain now. You don't know what it's like. You'll never know what it's like." After glancing at Edward, who did not react, he turned to Becka, "Becka-Lou, I'm sorry." But the girl couldn't see him as he began pacing back and forth. He looked away from his family. Edward was still there, still solemn.

Aevery shouted at Edward, "Can't you just leave me alone, man? Why don't you disappear and let me try and do something?"

"And what would that be?" Edward replied. "All you can do now is just watch everyone you love feel the consequences of your actions."

Candace picked up the phone again and dialed. "Sean?" She started to cry again. "Sorry to wake you, honey. You need to come over—it's your Dad."

Chapter Two

Cake and Cufflinks

Later that day, Aevery watched as the police arrived and filled his house with their investigation. They took scrapings from under his fingernails, samples of the debris on the bathroom wall, pictures of his body. They also took scrapings of under Candace and Becka's fingernails. People from the coroner's office carried his body to the gurney, wrapped it in a sheet, and covered it with a velvet cover.

Sean, Aevery and Candace's twenty-year-old son, and Becka consoled their mother as the gurney was carried down the stairs and rolled into the back of an unmarked white van. Later, Aevery watched as his body was rolled into a refrigerator drawer at the Coroner's Office. Edward, still in the background, stood silently.

That night, a New Age hippie named Janice, who was Aevery's sixty-year-old mother, was burning incense and meditating on a huge floor pillow, when he and Edward appeared in the living room of her apartment in Albuquerque, New Mexico. When her phone rang, Janice stretched across the floor to her purse, pulled out her phone, and answered it. Her son could hear both sides of the conversation.

"Janice? Hi, this is Candace."

"Candace? How are you? This is a surprise."

"I'm sorry, Janice, but I have some bad news."

"What is it?"

Candace paused, then said as calmly as she could, "Aevery is dead."

Janice gasped.

"He—he committed suicide this morning."

"Oh my God! What? Why?"

"I don't know. He had been struggling for a long time. Janice, I'm sorry. I…I have a lot to do. I'm sorry to tell you like this. Is there anyone I can call to come be with you?"

Janice looked bewildered, but she managed to say, "Sure, sure. I'm sure there's a lot to do. No, I'll be all right here. You don't need to call anyone."

Aevery rolled his eyes at Edward.

"I'll let you know about the memorial," Candace offered.

"You're having him cremated?"

Candace sounded a little impatient as she countered, "Like I said, Janice, he killed himself. Considering that, I think it's best he be cremated."

Janice still pressed to know more. "Oh—okay, I guess I didn't know what you meant."

"He shot himself. In the head."

Horror. Silence. Janice blinked through her tears. She had no idea what to say to her daughter-in-law.

Candace finally broke the silence. "I have to go now."

"Uh—of course. See you soon." Janice looked dazed as she ended the call. Then she really started to cry.

Aevery looked at Edward and shook his head like he didn't believe her.

"What's that look for?" asked Edward.

"She doesn't really care that much," Aevery told him.

"So you think she's just putting on?"

"Yeah," Aevery said, "All that? It's just an act."

Edward peered more closely at Aevery, "Who's she acting for? She's alone."

Aevery looked at his mother. "Well, she has never been there for me. Never was. She didn't come to my boot camp graduation. Never sent me a package while I was deployed." He looked angry and sad at the same time. "The only thing she ever did was send birthday and Christmas cards to the kids. Like twenty bucks is a good substitute for a grandma." He shook his head. "Thank God, Candace's mom and stepdad have been there for them." Then he leaned against the sofa and looked around the room as his mother cried.

Lots of people had gathered at the family home the next day. There was food, desserts, and lots of chatter. Candace sat in the living room, wearing dark glasses, just staring ahead. Several conversations took place, and Aevery got to hear all of them.

Gary, a neighbor, quietly spoke with his own wife, Susan. "What a jerk to do this to Candace. She's been such a good wife to him. Just 'cause he was 'having some problems'? Everyone has problems."

"I think there was more to it than that," Susan answered in a soft voice. She took a sip of her coffee. "Candace told me that they were having all sorts of financial problems—" she leaned in closer and covered one side of her mouth so no one else could hear, "—and some *other* problems, too." she said with one raised eyebrow. "He hadn't been right since he came back from Afghanistan."

Tony, Aevery's still-single, late-thirty something brother, looked around at the neighbors as he inched toward the stairs.

Aevery was the only one who noticed. "Tony, what the hell are you up to?" But Tony couldn't hear him, so Aevery followed him up the stairs.

Tony went into the master bedroom, peeked into the bathroom, gagged, and closed the door quickly but quietly. He took a look down the hall to see if anyone was coming, then hurried over to Candace's large, fancy, three-drawer jewelry box. He opened the third drawer, looked in, closed it, opened the second drawer, then the first, from which he snatched the diamond cufflinks.

"Tony—you jackass! What the hell are you doing?" Aevery tried to pull the diamonds out of Tony's hand, but his own hand went right through. "You drug-addled son-of-a-bitch! Those were Grandpa's, and they're to be handed down to my son!"

Without any reaction, Tony pocketed the loot, slipped back down the stairs, and blended back in with the guests.

Minutes later, Martha, Candace's snooty younger sister, sat down beside a cousin and spoke under her breath. "Well, if you ask me, I think the family—*the world really*—will be better off without him." She took a bite of cake, making sure to hold her hand so people could see her diamond rings. "I never did like him. I warned Candace not to marry him."

"Nobody fucking likes you, either," Aevery yelled in her ear. "Including Candace!"

Martha stopped. An odd look came over her. "Eww! I just got the chills, look, all the hair on my arm is standing up." She showed her cousin.

Aevery smirked. "Yep, and there's a lot of hair there; arms like a *fucking man.*"

Edward was staring at him.

"I just hate that!" Martha was saying. But the chills didn't bother her enough to make her stop eating. She took another bite of cake. Her diamonds sparkled again.

Aevery looked at Edward. "So, I just have to stand here and watch as everyone talks shit about me? While my memory is defiled and disgraced?"

Edward raised his eyebrows. "Well, they're just stating their feelings. Emotions run very high at times like these."

"Thank you for your pearls of wisdom. *Jesus!* I felt relieved for a while, but this just sucks!"

"I'm not Jesus," said the Guardian Angel. "The name is Edward. What can you do? Like I said—"

"—I know, I know. Just leave me alone, will ya?" Now Aevery was really mad.

Johannas, now also retired, leaned on his cane with one hand and sipped on his cup of coffee.

Sean was standing nearby. "Didn't you deploy with my dad?" he asked.

Johannas awkwardly transferred his cup to his cane hand so he could shake Sean's hand.

Sean tried to look away as his chin quivered. "Sorry, your strong handshake reminds me of my dad."

Johannas understood. "Son, your dad was quite a Marine. He really looked out for us."

Sean cleared his throat, "He never talked much about his deployments."

Johannas nodded. "Yeah, we saw some action in Iraq. I took a hit to my leg. I couldn't walk, so your dad helped me to the helicopter so they could evac me." His voice cracked. "Your dad was a good man. And a good Marine."

Aevery's attention turned back to his daughter, who was now standing by the table of desserts. She was wearing a black dress that was too tight, and her face was blotchy from crying so much. She poked a forkful of cake into her mouth. Every time someone walked up to her, she awkwardly set her paper plate down. When a friend of hers approached, she threw her plate into the trash.

At last, when people started to leave, Sean kissed his mother. Then he and his roommate Jake, Sean's best friend since high school, left. Edward and Aevery followed them.

Inside their small apartment, Sean turned on the TV and then went to sit close to Jake on the sofa. Aevery and Edward remained in the background. When Sean started to cry and laid his head on Jake's shoulder, the best friend put his arm around Sean and kissed his forehead.

"What th—?" Aevery looked at Edward, then back at Sean and Jake. "What the fuck is happening here? Oh, my God—no, not my son!" He turned back to Edward, "He's a fag?"

Edward merely waved one hand, and they were back at the wake. Air rushed past Aevery and Edward as they appeared in the kitchen.

"What the hell was that?" Aevery demanded.

"They needed some privacy."

"No, that's not what I meant! Trust me, I didn't want to stay there another minute! I mean, *what the fuck was that?*"

"Do I really need to spell it out for you?" Edward asked.

"I guess you do—and don't tell me my son is some sort of fucking faggot!"

"You won't ever hear those words come out of my mouth," Edward said.

"Oh, my God. It all makes sense to me now." Aevery nodded. "I always wondered why he never invited us over. They probably have women's underwear hanging all over the bathroom! That just makes me *SICK!*" He began pacing back and forth.

Edward was still calm. "That's a lot of judgment coming from you," he observed. Then he wrapped one arm around Aevery's shoulders and motioned to him that it was time to go, "Boy," he added, "are you in for some surprises."

"What the hell do you mean by that?"

"Oh, nothing. Just come with me."

But Aevery ducked and escaped from under Edward's arm. He pointed at his daughter. "And what is wrong with *her*?" She was still standing at the dessert table trying to eat another piece of cake.

"She's always been a good eater," he said, "but that's all she seems to want to do now. Can't she see she's fat? When did that happen?" He looked at Edward for an explanation and got none, so he looked back at Becka. "She needs to put that goddamned cake down and go for a run or something." Edward began pulling at him to go. "What's happening? My whole family is falling apart!"

Edward looked at him. "Oh, at last you're noticing what's going on with your family? That's good, considering you've been too preoccupied *and drunk* to notice much of anything for a long time." He picked at a piece of lint on Aevery's shirt. "And your son is not falling apart, he's just gay."

Aevery tried to smack Edward's hand, but his hand went right through. *"Don't touch me!"* He looked down at his shirt and brushed at something, then looked up at Edward. "My son laying his head on another man's shoulder," he batted his eyes like a girl, "and getting kissed gently on the forehead—" now a look of disgust washed over him. "That is the very definition of falling apart in my book!"

Edward came right back at him. "Yes, but we're not following your book anymore. You forfeited your book when you got drunk, took those pills, and decided to play Russian Roulette with yourself. Remember?" He gently tugged at Aevery. "It's time to go." Aevery avoided Edward's touch, but reluctantly went with him.

Edward waved his hand.

Air rushed past them as they appeared in the coroner's office exam room. Aevery's dead body was lying on a table with a sheet over it. The coroner's assistant was looking through a microscope, and the examiner had her hands in the open cavity of the body's upper torso.

"This guy must've had very high cholesterol," she said.

"How can you tell?" the assistant asked.

"Look at all the plaque."

They were hunched over his internal organs, probing with bloodied gloves. Now Aevery looked in, too.

"Suicide is so sad," the assistant said.

"Well, this guy was probably well on his way to a heart attack, anyway. It's a shame. Looks like he wasn't too bad looking—before he blew his brains out, that is. And check out the size of his—" she looked at the assistant and gestured at his lower half.

The assistant looked under the sheet. "Whoa. Impressive."

Aevery had to speak up. "Yep. I was always proud of the little guy. Too bad he didn't work that well for the last few years. You should've seen us in our heyday, though."

Edward gave him a forced smile.

Sometime later at the mortuary, Aevery watched

and Edward stood by as his body was shoved into the cremation retort.

Aevery and Edward accompanied Candace to the mortuary the next day. She was still wearing dark glasses. "I'm here to pick up my husband," she said. "Uh, I mean his remains." She signed some papers and they gave her the box in a velvet bag. She looked at it, finding it very hard to believe this was all that was left of her husband the Marine. The young man who had stood with her in his dress blues at their marriage. The man who had fought for his country. The man who had fathered her children and read bedtime stories to them. The man who had been both her lover and best friend and had cried when he found out she had miscarried their third baby. She carefully picked up the box in the velvet bag and slowly walked out.

"So," Aevery said, "as you can see, Candace didn't want to buy one of those fancy urns. I guess she's just gonna put me in the closet with our matching bowling balls."

"That sounds like a good idea," Edward said, slapping Aevery on the back and making him lurch forward. The deceased Marine was a tad offended. They walked out to the car with Candace. Aevery sat in the passenger seat, Edward in the back.

Candace, in the driver's seat, began crying and talking to the box in her lap. "Why did you do this, you selfish bastard? Why did you leave me? I thought we were in this together. 'Til death do us part, not 'til you decide death do us part! Dammit!" She flung the box onto the passenger seat, where it went right through Aevery. He looked at it. She pounded on the steering wheel, then looked down at the box and slapped it. "Son-of-a-bitch!" It tumbled to the floor in front of the seat.

Aevery just sat there with his cremains at his feet. There wasn't much else he could do. "If I had it to do over again," he muttered. "Yeah, I should've gone to a shrink, taken some meds, I should've tried harder at life. Maybe cared more about my family." He looked down at his fingernails and sighed. "I just wanted out… I thought everyone would be better off without me. And I was in pain, you know. Lots and lots of pain."

A week later, Aevery and Edward stood just inside the doors of the church and watched as family and friends filed in for Aevery's memorial service. People hugged each other and wiped tears away, they kissed Becka and Sean and told them how sorry they were. Janice took a seat by herself, off to one side of the church, away from the family.

As the priest began the Mass, an unkempt Tony skulked in and sank into one of the back pews.

"Tony," Aevery said as soon as he noticed his brother, "you're worthless. Someday you'll be late to your own funeral." Candace stared ahead, stone-faced, ignoring her brother-in-law.

After the opening prayer, Sean stood up and walked to the lectern carrying a fistful of papers. He took a place next to his father's last promotion portrait, a huge floral wreath, and the box of cremains. After adjusting the microphone, he awkwardly cleared his throat. "My father joined the Marines when he was nineteen. He finally retired after serving twenty-two years." He glanced at his father's big photograph. "We went with him as he changed duty stations six times in his career. We got to live at several different Marine bases." He looked out at the audience and smiled. He was trying to give a good speech. "We spent time in Okinawa, in Hawaii, in North Carolina, and in Twentynine Palms and Oceanside, California. And, of course, here in Quantico. This is where Dad decided he wanted to retire. He was a fine, upstanding Marine. We are very proud of him, and we will miss him very much." Looking relieved, Sean bowed his head briefly, then returned to sit with Jake.

Aevery looked at Edward. "That's it? That's all? I was just a good Marine? What about what a good person I was? What a good father I was? Husband, son, brother?" He marched to the altar, turned, and shouted at the congregation. "There was NOTHING to my life before the Marine Corps, huh? Nothing afterwards? COME ON. Isn't anyone else going to say anything? MOM? *Come on!*" But they could neither see nor hear him.

Edward was becoming annoyed. "In Sean's

defense," he said, "that's all he's ever known. You as a Marine. He's probably the only one here that could muster up the strength to give your eulogy. Give him a break."

That night, as Candace slept in a makeshift bed at her mother's house, Aevery sat down next to her and tried to whisper in her ear. "Candace, I'm still here. Candace, I love you."

She started to cry.

"Candace please forgive me. You don't know the pain I was in."

She began crying harder, then woke up, sat upright, and screamed, "No! I won't forgive you, you selfish son-of-a-bitch! You should've gotten help!" She buried her head in her hands and cried some more.

Candace's mother, Alice hurried in. "What is it, dear?"

"I saw him in a dream. He asked me to forgive him!" Candace began sobbing into her mother's shoulder.

Aevery looked at Edward. "So she heard me?!"

"Yes," Edward answered. "Sometimes spirits can connect with people in the dreamtime. The channel has less interference while they're sleeping."

Aevery looked happily at Candace.

Becka came in. "Mom, what's wrong? Grandma, what happened?"

"It's okay, dear," Alice said. "Your mother just had a bad dream. Go back to bed, sweetie. I'll come and tuck you in."

CHAPTER THREE

A MASSACRE

Edward and Aevery next came to the entryway of a huge hall that had brilliantly polished floors and seemed to have no end. There was no ceiling, only clouds. U.S. Marines stood guard along the hall.

"Where are we?" Aevery asked. "What is this?"

With no apparent end to his patience, Edward responded, "This is the Great Hall of the Akashic Records."

"What are Akashic Records?"

"The Records are like filmstrips or tapes of people's lives."

"Oh—you guys haven't gone digital yet, huh?"

Edward, less than amused, just stared at him.

Of course, Aevery had another question. "So, I suppose every little thing I've ever done is recorded here?"

Edward smiled. "Not exactly. But we do have a

lot of filmstrip rolls on you." He laughed at his own joke a little too much for Aevery's comfort, then patted Aevery on the back and nudged him forward toward a man who was dressed in a World War II USMC uniform and standing at a huge, gilded, reception desk.

"Hello," the man said in a no-nonsense tone. "I'm Rowan, one of the Archivists."

"Where is my family?" Aevery inquired. "I thought I'd get to see my Nana. And I'd love to finally meet my Grandpa. Where are they?"

"Aevery, you must be patient," Rowan replied. "All of this takes time. You have all eternity to see your family. But first you must be counseled."

"*Counseled?* I just want to see my family." He looked around and called, "Nana? Grandpa?"

"You are just prolonging the inevitable." Edward pushed him in the direction he wanted him to go. "Let's go."

Aevery called out again, "Nana? Grandpa?" His voice echoed in the great hall.

"This one is spirited, isn't he?" Rowan observed.

"He was a Marine," Edward replied.

"Once a Marine, *always a Marine!*" Aevery nearly shouted.

Edward conceded the truth of that and nodded to Rowan. "Okay, he *is* a Marine." Then he pushed Aevery again. They walked forward together.

Finally allowing himself to be redirected, Aevery turned to his Guardian Angel and asked,

"Edward, what's an Archivist?"

"They hold the records of all your past lives. Everybody's, in fact. You have to be counseled. Everyone does when they cross over to the Other Side." Edward was walking with his hand on Aevery's shoulder.

"So I gotta have therapy?" Aevery asked sarcastically.

"Not exactly. It's more like a life review. Key moments. Instant replays. The director's cut." Edward shrugged. "However you want to look at it."

When they entered the Library itself, Aevery saw huge bookshelves that went clear up to the sky holding golden books. He saw windows that went up as far up as the eye could see and showed the twinkling stars and clouds of the night. Edward invited Aevery to sit down. He located the correct filmstrip canister and handed it to Aevery.

"What's this?" Aevery asked.

"It's one of your Akashic Records."

"What will I find in there?"

"Your history." A serious look came over Edward's face. "I want to show you that you've always tended to bail out when the going gets tough."

Aevery glared at him. "How the hell would you know that?"

"You and I have traveled together before."

"You'll have to show me, then, because I don't

understand what the fuck you're talking about."

"It's all in there," Edward said in his customary patient tone. "Open it."

Aevery opened the lid of the canister and pulled out the filmstrip. As he unrolled it, light shone from it and lit up his face. He felt wind blowing his hair.

Edward waved his hand.

Now sitting in complete darkness, Aevery could still hear Edward speaking. "The time we need to go back to," he was saying, "is a few centuries ago—one of our many lives together. Tony was your older brother in this Tribe."

"What do you mean 'our lives together'?" Aevery asked into the nothingness.

"I've been your Guardian Angel through many different incarnations." Edward's words echoed through the ethers.

Aevery suddenly found himself in the body of a little Native American boy in a large wigwam. He was sitting next to his older brother in a circle of children younger and older than him. Everyone spoke in their native language, which Aevery could understand. The smells of the earthen floor and the fire were very strong. They were sitting in a circle for story time, and they giggled and poked at each other until an older girl child corrected the boys. Then they paid attention, knowing they had better mind out of respect to the storyteller.

An instant passed, and now Aevery was a young teenage boy, using a spear to fish in a deep stream. His brother, Tony again, was walking along a huge fallen log. He suddenly lost his balance and fell into the water. Aevery laughed at him and told him that the Fallen Standing Person, as Native Americans refer to trees, had thrown him.

Another instant passed, and now Aevery was a young adult wearing his finest skins and standing before the tribe. Beside him stood a ceremonially adorned young maiden. They were about to be married. Tony proudly looked on. The scene flickered in Aevery's mind between this young maiden and Candace on their wedding day. He looked down at his arms and chest and saw them flicker between the buckskin and his Alpha Dress Blue uniform. His bride's hands rested in his and felt comfortable and familiar. He looked down at their joined hands and saw Candace's wedding rings flickering on and off the maiden's hand.

Before he knew it, he and his young wife were in a wigwam at night. He could smell the moisture in the air, the approach of fall. And blood. She had just given birth. She handed Aevery the baby. Just then, as he reached for his son, the scene flickered between Native American Candace and modern-day Candace. When he looked down at his baby, the image he saw flickered between the Native American baby and baby Sean. Chills slowly enveloped his body as he recognized the familiarity in the eyes of his wife and newborn son. He knew they were the same people who had been in his current life. On the deepest sensory level, he knew, as he had never known before.

Then Aevery found himself walking through the forest with Tony. They were carrying several dead rabbits, and the smells of blood, skunk, and pine filled his senses. Just then, another smell intruded—the smell of smoke. They could see it in the distance. They began running. Aevery felt scared and nauseated. When they reached the top of the mountain, they saw their village was on fire. Still running, Aevery and Tony slid down the hill as fast as they could into the village. They looked around at all the slaughtered people. Women, children, and elders all lay dead. Aevery was frantic. When he found the bodies of his wife and baby, he fell on top of them, in tears and searched them for any signs of life. He lifted his wife and shook her, screaming at her to live. That's when he felt the blood all over her back. He also picked up his blood-soaked baby and screamed again.

Tears streamed down Aevery's face as he looked at Tony, whose image flickered between his Native American brother and his drug-addled modern brother. He felt air rushing through his head and broke away from the reality he was facing. He could no longer cope with what had happened, and lit out, running away from the village, faster and faster through the forest, with Tony right behind and shouting after him. He climbed higher and higher into the mountains, his feet slipping on the underbrush and rocks, making him scramble even harder. The higher he got, the more his brother shouted after him. At the summit of the mountain, he looked back, caught his brother's eyes in the distance, and then surrendered, letting himself fall backwards off the cliff. Tony stopped at the edge of the cliff and fell to his knees, defeated. The last thing Aevery heard was his brother's screams, begging not to be left alone.

Aevery was once again in darkness. A voice came from the ethers. "You had no idea how this would affect anyone but yourself," Edward explained. "You left your brother there to carry on all alone. With your suicide, his whole family was dead."

Aevery was brought out of the darkness long enough to see his brother crying over his dead body. Then he was again engulfed in the darkness.

Edward's voice again split the ethers. "And that wasn't the last time you abandoned him."

Air rushed past as Edward and Aevery appeared in the kitchen of his boyhood home. They stood to one side and watched what was happening. Young Janice, in her thirties, tearfully hugged a thirteen-year-old Tony, who was also in tears. Aevery immediately recalled the year: 1991. A younger version of him came into the kitchen with a suitcase.

Young Janice turned to him. "After your grandfather died in Vietnam, you're still going to enlist? You know this goes against everything I believe in. We need you here. Son, I need your help!"

Rage welled up in the young Aevery, and he almost shouted as he pushed past them, "It's not my fault he hasn't got a father. I've gotta go. You're both on your own now. Say goodbye to Nana for me."

Young Tony, obviously feeling that old, familiar feeling of being at his brother's mercy, couldn't bear to see him leave. "Please don't leave me again," he begged.

"What do you mean 'again'? You'll be all right, won't you, kid?" Young Aevery mussed Young Tony's hair and kissed his mother on the cheek. Then he walked toward the door. Suddenly he turned back to her. "Mom, I'm sick and tired of just dreaming. I *have* to do this. I wanna make something of myself." As he turned toward the door again, he tried to keep his emotions from welling up, but he couldn't. He blinked back his tears. Despite the conflicting but compelling urge to stay, he left.

Edward looked at Aevery and waved his hand.

Aevery and Edward were now transported to the Military Entrance Processing Station (MEPS). It was later that same day. Every Marine, no matter his or her rank, had Young Aevery's attention now. He so looked up to them that he wanted to be just like them. As young Aevery sat reading his enlistment paperwork, another version of Edward stood behind him, shaking his head.

Young Aevery, who hadn't signed the papers yet, looked puzzled. "I wish someone would tell me what to do," he said under his breath.

Just then, the other Edward pushed the paperwork off the desk. Young Aevery picked it up, looked around, and hastily signed it.

Edward looked at Aevery, "You had a gut feeling you were doing the wrong thing. But you ignored that message from the Divine."

Later that day, Young Aevery stood in line to be processed. Now the other Edward had incarnated and was dressed as a Marine to get Young Aevery's attention. When he walked through the line and ran into Young Aevery, the paperwork fell to the floor.

"Oh, I'm sorry," Incarnated Edward said. "Let me help you."

"No. I got it."

Aevery looked at Edward. "I remember that! That was you? You ran into me. How could you be solid like that?"

Edward grinned. "We can materialize at times if

we wish, usually in *dire circumstances*."

Aevery was now annoyed, "Well, if you thought my enlisting was such a bad idea, why didn't you just say, 'Hey, man! You're making a mistake! Don't do this'?"

"That would have been tampering with your free will," Edward said matter-of-factly. "Something we are not allowed to do." He looked intently at Aevery. "It seems like, since then, ever since you enlisted, you have made it a point to purposefully ignore your Divine Gut," he pointed at Spirit Aevery's solar plexus. "Why is that?"

Aevery rolled his eyes.

Edward looked at him again in all seriousness, and the scene faded from gray to pitch black. Edward's voice cut through the quiet darkness. "It was just two years later that Tony tried heroin for the first time. He was only fifteen. Maybe if you would've waited to enlist until he graduated from high school, things might've been very different."

Chapter Four

Curiosity in the Creek

Aevery again found himself back in the Library of the Great Hall of Records. "I'm done here!" he shouted at Edward. "*I'm done!* I don't want to see any more!" He reached toward Edward, but his hands couldn't grasp the Guardian Angel.

Edward was now wearing a World War I Drill Instructor's uniform. He grabbed Aevery firmly by the collar and shook him. Aevery looked surprised and a little startled. He felt like he was right back in boot camp. Edward shouted in Aevery's face, "You chose this life for yourself! You can't change it!" He grabbed him even tighter until they were nose to nose. The brim of Edward's hat nearly touched Aevery's forehead. "This is what you did to others around you! Stop trying to deny what you've done!"

"Easy for you to point fingers," Aevery sneered. "Have you ever been human?"

Edward loosened his grip. "No, I've never been human."

"So how would you know the effects I've had on anyone?"

"Because I've been with you through all of it."

Aevery pressed his advantage and looked Edward up and down, "So if you've never been human, you've never been a Marine. So why have you been wearing our uniforms, then? You don't rate to wear them." He leaned in on Edward.

"Marines are the only human beings you respect. That's why."

Aevery, chin up, looked away, proudly. "That's right! So where do we go from here, Mister Know-It-All?" But when he turned to look, Edward was now wearing a biblical robe. He looked like an Angel, his huge, magnificent wings glistening in the light. Aevery couldn't hide that he was awestruck, but then he slipped right back into smart-ass. "What's with the robe, man?"

"Don't you recognize me from Catechism?" Edward assumed the posture of an Angel in a painting, wings outstretched. A soft breeze blew his hair and rippled his robe. There was a mischievous twinkle in his eyes.

Aevery just looked at him. "Oh, brother."

"Isn't this what you would expect me to look like?"

Aevery shook his head, so Edward changed form again. Now he was still wearing the robe, but he had no wings. There was a golden halo around his head, as saints are portrayed in paintings. "Is this better?"

"No. I liked the wings better."

"Wings it is, then." Edward changed again: wings but no halo. "Now that we're in agreement about my appearance, are you ready to begin again?"

Aevery sighed, "Oh, God, how much more?"

"I'm not God."

Aevery rolled his eyes.

Edward smiled. "Centuries more."

Edward pointed to a pile of filmstrips on the library table, then unrolled another one and waved his hand.

Aevery was again engulfed in darkness. He could hear water moving and smell forest leaves. The smell of the forest reminded him of the forest near his home in Virginia. As the darkness faded, he looked down at himself and discovered he was now in the body of a twenty-four-year-old man wearing a Union Army uniform of what looked to be the Civil War era. He was now marching alongside a slightly younger man he knew to be his brother Tony and another young man named Bosen. Suddenly he knew the year was 1864. He also knew his name and rank. He knew about his family. He knew he liked to write letters home to his mother, but he almost hated his overbearing father.

The men were tired from having marched with their regiment all day. They smelled of sweat and dust. When they were dismissed, Aevery, Tony, and Bosen split off from the rest and began to undress by the creek. Tony quickly escaped the confines of his uniform and took his clothes with him when he jumped in. Bosen and Aevery undressed a tad more slowly. They could see other soldiers upstream also undressing and bathing in the deep creek.

As Aevery undressed, Bosen tried not to look, but couldn't help but glance awkwardly at him. Aevery noticed. By this time Tony was getting out on the other side of the creek. He wrung out his clothes and started to climb a tree to hang them on a branch.

Aevery and Bosen got in the water together. Aevery was curious about Bosen and swam closer to him. "I noticed you looking at me," Aevery said almost under his breath.

Bosen flushed with embarrassment and moved his arms around in the water. He knew that Aevery could make a lot of trouble for him. Fear welled up inside as he said, "I—I beg your pardon. Please don't tell anyone—"

Aevery smiled. "—I don't take offense." He moved closer to Bosen and lightly touched his stomach. Bosen gasped with pleasure. His hand moved slowly down to feel Bosen's erection. He didn't resist. Aevery moved in for a kiss. Their lips barely touched, but Bosen pulled away.

They didn't know it, but Tony was watching from the tree, where he was still arranging his clothes. He saw everything. Bosen looked up and down the creek, saw no one close, then quickly moved in, and gently grabbed Aevery by the sides of his face. They shared a very passionate kiss, which startled Tony so much he let out a yelp and fell out of the tree. Aevery and Bosen moved away from each other.

Edward brought Aevery's consciousness back to the Great Library.

He glared at Edward, *"Oh. My. Fucking. God!* Why in God's name did you have to show me *that*?"

Edward merely grinned. "Talk about gays in the military…"

"No. I'm serious! I could've lived a thousand more years without knowing I was a gay soldier in the Civil War."

"You're so judgmental about your son, I needed you to see how you once lived."

The filmstrip picked up where it had left off.

Aevery was back in the Civil War. That night, the three men ate their dinners around the small bivouac fire and other soldiers milled about. Bosen finished and got up. As he walked away, Tony whispered to Aevery, "Please tell me I didn't see what I saw at the creek."

Aevery was tired of his brother's watchful eyes. "Dear brother, whatever are you talking about?"

"That kiss?"

Aevery took another bite of food. "Brother, you've known since we were children that I don't fancy the ladies."

"Well, you had better watch yourself, *dear brother*, so father doesn't find out." Tony put his food down, stood up, and looked down at Aevery. "Have you forgotten the beating?"

Aevery looked around to see if anyone heard. "Sit down, you fool! No need to attract attention."

Tony reluctantly sat back down and picked up his plate.

Aevery's interest in boys in his mid-19th-century life had always been a family secret. Everyone knew it, though they denied it. He remembered his father's rage as he'd beat him with a razor strop until he had a split lip and a black eye and was not able to sit down for several days. Aevery's father believed that his son's interest in boys was a choice that could be beaten out of him. He also remembered his mother crying as she tended his wounds.

"No, I have not forgotten," Aevery whispered, trying to contain his anger, "but I am no longer a boy. I no longer care what father thinks. I cannot change who I am."

Tony became sullen and quietly angry, though he said nothing.

"And now let me warn you, little brother," Aevery said, staring at Tony, "you would be wise not to arouse my anger."

Aevery felt the movement of air around him. He was back in the Library, still angry, but also a little chagrined when he saw Edward. "So," he said, "I suppose we settled down and decorated a little dirt-floor love nest together?"

"No," Edward replied, "you'll see."

The Battle of Spotsylvania Courthouse was fought a few days later in a large field where Union soldiers charged Confederate soldiers. Bullets flew, and canons fired. The soldiers engaged in hand-to-hand combat. The smell of gunpowder and death overwhelmed Aevery's senses. Aevery and Bosen stayed close to each other. A Confederate soldier they couldn't see through the smoke charged at them and stabbed Bosen in the stomach with his bayonet. As Bosen collapsed on the grass, Aevery hit the Confederate soldier across the face with the butt of his rifle. Bosen lay near death, his mouth filled with blood. Just then, a bullet hit Aevery in the chest. He fell face down near his newfound love and reached for Bosen's hand across the bloodstained grass. Another Confederate soldier stabbed Aevery in the back with his bayonet, killing him. The two men lay dead, hand in hand.

Aevery longed for this memory to come to an end. So much of it was making him uncomfortable. Touching another man, too much blood, the familiar stench of death—all these reduced Aevery to tears. The joy of those few short days with Bosen came flooding back to him. A man had returned his affections. To witness his death was unbearable. He welcomed his own death.

Now, grateful the experience was over, he

waited for the signal that it was done.

After the familiar rush of air, Aevery found himself back in the great Library, still shaken and sitting in a chair.

"What's the matter?" Edward asked. "Loved him, did you?"

Aevery sniffled, tears still in his eyes. "Let's just move it along, shall we?"

Edward patted him gently on the shoulder. "Now we get to see some really interesting stuff."

Aevery shook off his Civil War incarnation as if it were only a vivid dream. When he'd regained his composure, he looked up at Edward. "You're really enjoying this, aren't you?"

Edward smiled reassuringly. "This won't be so bad. What is it you Marines say all the time? 'Hurry up and wait'? Something like that?"

Aevery crossed his arms, sighed and surrendered.

Edward picked up another filmstrip.

Chapter Five

A Shirt with Flowers

The darkness was only a few moments old when Aevery found himself aboard a Marine Base. It was 2003, and he was walking arm in arm with Candace and holding a four-year-old Becka in his arms. Beside them skipped a seven-year-old Sean, who was dressed in a flowery polo shirt. Aevery recalled having just stepped off the bus from a deployment. Aevery finally sat down, still holding Becka. Sean hugged him, which is when he noticed the shirt.

Aevery pointed. "Did you pick out that shirt?" he asked Candace. "He looks gay." Sean looked down at his shirt.

"Dear God, Aevery!" Candace bellowed.

Aevery tried to distract Sean by saying, "Stand up straight, son." Sean stood up straighter. Candace, still angry, raked Sean's hair with her fingertips.

Aevery looked around, purposely avoiding Candace's gaze. "I wonder if they've got beer here.

I'm gonna go look." He stood up and walked away from his family.

Aevery felt the familiar rush of air, which fluffed his hair. Back at the Library, he looked up to see Edward looking down at him.

"What? I needed a beer. We couldn't drink the whole time we were deployed."

"You know that's not the issue," Edward said.

"Well, that was *the gayest* shirt I've ever seen. He looked like he'd just walked out of an episode of *The Brady Bunch* or something.

Edward looked dumbfounded. "Wow. And you still can't bring yourself to admit you were wrong? Your son wanted to look nice for you. That was a seven-year-old's idea of a fancy shirt."

"Okay! Okay! God, when you get something stuck in your—"

"—I told you. I'm not God, or Jesus. I'm Edward."

"Har har har. Okay, so I said some insensitive things to the boy. I guess I was trying to toughen him up." He looked up. Edward stared right back at him. "I. Was. Wrong. Okay? There, I said it. You happy now?"

Edward was obviously not happy. "You know what? Your son did the best he could with you being gone through most of his formative years."

"Oh, so now you want to lay a guilt trip on me?"

"What did you expect? Did you expect Tony to

be a good role model for your son? What male role model did he have besides you?"

"So I turned him gay," Aevery said sarcastically, "by criticizing his gay shirt."

"Your son was born gay." Edward picked up another filmstrip canister from the pile.

"Stop it!" Aevery tried to grab the new filmstrip from Edward, but again his hand went right through.

On the other side of the rush of air, Aevery found himself and Candace standing in their living room taking pictures of an exasperated Sean, age seventeen now and dressed in a navy-blue tuxedo, standing with his date for the senior prom. It was now 2013. Eighteen-year-old Jake was standing with his date too.

Sean was embarrassed by all the fuss Candace was making. "Geez, Mom, how many pictures you gonna take?"

Candace reviewed the pictures she had taken so far. "Sean, you look like you're about to go in front of a firing squad. It wouldn't kill you to smile, you know."

Sean forced a smile.

"That's better, sweetie." Candace took a few more shots.

Aevery leaned closer to his wife and whispered, "If he turns out to be gay, I'm gonna shoot myself."

Candace couldn't hide the fact that she knew

something, but merely gave her husband a half-hearted smile. "How can you say that?"

He was almost instantly transported back to the Library. His hair hadn't finished fluffing yet as he turned to Edward and shouted, "Why do you have to show me all this shit? Don't you think I know I was an asshole? My God! I don't want to see this, I don't wanna go on."

Edward walked away. "And you wondered why no one could come up with something good to say about you at your funeral?" He walked back to Aevery, carrying another filmstrip from a different part of the Library. "I have one I want you to see that doesn't involve you. We are just going to visit this one."

"Thank God."

When the darkness cleared, it was 1932, the worst year of the Great Depression. A twenty-something woman named Anna was standing with her four-year-old daughter, Becky, in the living room of a modest little house. Becky, who seemed scared, looked up at her mother.

Edward and Aevery were watching from the background. Edward turned to Aevery and whispered, "That was your Becka in her last life."

A doctor came out of the bedroom. There was a grim look on his face.

"How is he, Doctor?" Anna asked.

The doctor looked shaken. "Not good, I'm afraid. The tree that fell on him shoved a branch right into his leg. I'm afraid he won't be able to work for quite a while."

Anna started to cry.

Time passed, and now Edward and Aevery were watching Anna and Becky in the kitchen.

Little Becky was sitting at the table. "I'm hungry, Momma."

"I know, sweetie, I am, too." Anna choked back her tears, trying to be strong for her girl. "We have to give all the food to Daddy so he can get better." She gave Becky three soda crackers. "Here, sweetie, I know it isn't much, but it's all we have."

"Thank you, Momma." Becky took a bite of the first soda cracker. "You know what, Momma?"

"What, angel?"

"When we get money again, I want to have cake *every day*."

Anna chuckled through her tears. "I do, too, sweetie."

Now, back at the Library, Aevery thought that the air had transported them back prematurely. He looked at Edward. "Well? What happened?"

"She died of malnutrition within a year."

"She didn't survive? She didn't survive?" Aevery felt himself becoming emotional. "Oh. My. God! And that was my Becka?"

Edward put his hand on Aevery's shoulder. As Aevery openly cried, the Guardian Angel picked up another filmstrip.

At this point, Aevery didn't even protest. Air rushed past, and soon they were back in 2003 in the kitchen of his and Candace's first house. The whole family was gathered around Becka, who faced a birthday cake with a big "4" candle on it. She blew out the candle, very excited at the prospect of having cake. She watched with eager anticipation as it was cut and served.

"Daddy, you know what I wished for when I blew out the candle?" Becka said, her voice quivering with excitement.

"What, sweetheart?"

"I wished I could have cake *every day*!"

They all laughed.

This time, Aevery was relieved to feel the rush of air. He found himself sitting in a chair again, tears streaming down his cheeks. "I always wondered why food was so important to her," he muttered. "I always saw it as weakness."

"What you see in this life is a carryover from that life," Edward replied. "Her soul remembers and pushes her to make sure she never experiences hunger or starvation again." After a pause, he patted Aevery on the back and smiled. "Are you ready to move on to your mother?"

Aevery looked at him, shocked, "Oh, come on!" As Edward went into another section of the Library, he wiped his face, sniffled, and called after him. "Haven't I been through enough? I won't see anything there that'll make me feel any different!"

Edward walked back carrying two more filmstrip canisters. "We'll see," he said. As he unrolled a new filmstrip, light shone from it.

Chapter Six

Mom's Therapy

A new swoosh of air sent Edward and Aevery to the well-decorated office of Janice's therapist. It was 2013, and they were in Albuquerque, New Mexico. Janice, seated in a large, comfortable chair, was in the middle of a session. Dana, the therapist, who was in her fifties and wore glasses, sat facing her client and took careful notes as Janice talked through her tears. Edward and Aevery stood in the corner and listened.

"My son, Aevery," Janice was saying, "has just retired from the Marine Corps. But he's made it clear he doesn't want to talk to me. I always hoped our relationship would get better, not worse."

Dana looked up and took off her glasses. "What would you want your son to know if he was here right now?"

Janice thought for a minute, looked around the room, and said, "I'd want him to know that I've always loved him. That I've always been proud of his military career, but…well, it was my stubbornness that got in the way."

"How?"

"Well, I was at his graduation from boot camp, but I couldn't bring myself to go up and congratulate him. I didn't even tell my mother." She looked down at her hands.

"Why not?"

Janice leaned forward. "Well…the last thing I wanted was for my son to go into the Marine Corps. Even though men in my family have always been in the military." She shook her head. "I wasn't the most popular person in my family, you know, when I was protesting a war that my dad died in. And then…two pregnancies, out of wedlock, within six years?" She took a deep breath. "It's funny. When you have a child, you think 'everything's gonna be fine, we'll see eye to eye on everything, and our future will be peachy-keen.' You never expect the worst."

"Was Aevery's enlisting the worst?"

"No, I think this is the worst. On top of all that, now I've lost my son to war-related PTSD and alcoholism." She began sobbing violently. "And the goddam military machine just keeps chugging along."

The therapist set a box of tissues down on the table in front of her.

Janice took a few tissues. "I just couldn't believe

my son would defy me like that."

"Do you really think he was defying you by enlisting?"

"Yes, I do. I saw it as him being sick and tired of my anti-war talk all his young life. This was the most rebellious thing he could do to get back at me."

Aevery looked at his mother. "Oh. My. God! Really, Mom? Really?"

Dana furrowed her brow. "Oh, really?"

"I know, even as I'm saying it," Janice admitted, "it sounds awful." She blew her nose.

"Were you rebelling against your own mother while you were protesting the war?" Dana asked.

Janice thought a moment. "Yes. It was definitely rebellion on my part."

"So…when you were rebelling, how did you feel about it?"

"Well, I knew I was right. I didn't really care what my mother thought." Janice looked squarely at her therapist. "I have never been able to hang with that old us-against-them mentality. We are *all one*, so why must we fight?"

"Do you think Aevery could've felt driven, somehow, to be a Marine? Kind of like you were driven to be an anti-war protester?"

Janice looked surprised, as if a light bulb had just turned on in her head. "You know—I never thought of it that way! I just thought he was being a little shit and wanted to defy me."

Dana permitted herself a smile. "Sounds like the

apple didn't fall far from the tree. You two actually have a lot in common." She jotted a few notes, then looked up and said, "What else would you say to him?"

That's when Janice broke down again. "I would say, 'I'm sorry, son. I'm sorry for what I said when you were leaving for boot camp. Instead of using your brother as an excuse, I should've said—'" she had to take a huge breath "—I should've said, 'Hey, son, I don't want to see you in a coffin like I had to see my dad. I don't want you to gamble with your life, because I love you too much.'"

Dana moved the box of tissues closer to Janice. "If he heard you say that, how do you think he would react?"

Janice could only shake her head. "I don't know. But at least he would've gone to boot camp knowing his mother loved him and just couldn't get past losing her dad." She grabbed a handful of tissues and began crying into them. "And if I could go back again, I'd congratulate him for becoming a Marine. I will *always* regret not showing him I was there."

Therapist Dana, who was on the verge of tearing up herself, took a sip of water to calm her reaction. "Do you think," she began in a soft voice, "do you think there may be a time when you can forgive yourself?"

Janice breathed deeply. "I don't know. That's a hard one. And my guilt has made me not even try to get close to my grandkids. You know they're teenagers now." She fiddled with the tissues in her hands. "Thinking about that makes me feel even worse."

"Sounds like you've been carrying a lot of guilt and regret for a long time."

"I just wish things could be different. I wish we could understand each other."

"Do you think that would be possible? And he might be willing to talk about it?"

"Janice looked down at her hands again. "Maybe. If he sobered up." She took another deep breath. "I would try to talk to him if he was in recovery."

Another rush of air, and Aevery and Edward were back in the Library.

"Wow," Aevery was muttering, "I never dreamed she had all that bottled up inside her."

Edward was already holding another filmstrip. "Now I want you to see, firsthand, what happened back then."

The smell of the outdoors, especially the freshly cut grass, overwhelmed Aevery's senses. They were standing in the Los Angeles National Cemetery. The year was 1970. A fourteen-year-old Janice was sitting with her mother, Carol. Both were dressed in black. Petty Officer 2nd Class Paul Warrier's military funeral was just ending. Young men from the United States Navy had just removed the flag from the coffin and were folding it.

A young Petty Officer 2nd Class handed the folded flag to Carol. "On behalf of the President of the United States and the Chief of Naval Operations, please accept this flag as a symbol of our appreciation for your loved one's service to this Country and a grateful Navy. God bless you and this family, and God bless the United States of America." He stepped back, stood at attention, and saluted her.

Carol was sobbing, her hands covering her mouth. Janice cried, too, and tried to comfort her mother.

Chapter Seven

An Unexpected Reunion

This time, when the rush of air passed over them, Aevery and Edward were standing on a dark shoreline.

Aevery wiped at a tear. "I had no idea," he murmured. "I just always thought she was being a bitch."

Edward patted him on the back. "That's the reason I wanted you to see that funeral."

There was no moon in the sky. The only light shown from an old-fashioned lantern that hung from the bow of a large, gondola-like boat that was beached nearby. Edward motioned for Aevery to get aboard.

"What's this?" Aevery asked, "Where are we going now?" He climbed aboard. Edward followed.

"I'm taking you to the place of your Ancestors." He shoved off with a long oar.

The water was like glass. The warm ocean breeze felt good on Aevery's face, but the moonless sky made him feel uneasy. Edward was rowing. They were still in total darkness except for the light of the lantern. Soon Aevery began to see a shiny island in the distance. The sticky salt sea air whipped Aevery's hair. He looked around. "Where is the moon?"

"This sea never sees the light of the sun. Nor the moon," Edward told him. "That's why it's called The Sunless Sea."

"I can't wait to see Nana. Sweetest lady who ever lived. And I hope I finally get to meet Grandpa."

"I hope they're available," Edward said.

"How could they not be available? Trust me. They'll want to see me."

The journey to the Shining Isle was smooth and uneventful, and before Aevery knew it, they were dragging the boat out of the water. It was still night on the beach, but there was light in the distance.

Once the boat was beached, Edward turned to Aevery, "You ready?"

"Let's go."

As they walked through a patch of forest, the distant light became brighter and brighter. When they came to a large guard post manned by U.S. Marines, Edward rubbed his thumb and fingers together and a badge appeared in his hand. He showed the guards his credentials, and they were both waved through.

Surprised, Aevery exclaimed, "I'll be a son-of-a-bitch! The Marine Corps Hymn is right!" He remembered the end of the Hymn: *If the Army and the Navy/ Ever look on Heaven's scenes,/ They will find the streets are guarded/ By United States Marines.*

Once they were past the guard post, it was daytime and Edward and Aevery found themselves in the middle of an apple orchard. The trees had blossoms and fruit at the same time, and petals rained down on them in a cool perfumed breeze.

A crowd of people were standing in the distance, apparently waiting for Aevery. When he came closer, he saw Aunt Hazel and Uncle Richard standing in front of his grandparents, Carol and Paul Warrier, who looked very polished in his Navy dress whites. When Aevery realized what and who he was looking at, he couldn't help but tearing up and running toward them. Everyone was thrilled to see him. They hugged him and caressed his face.

"Aunt Hazel," he nearly shouted, "look at you! So good to see you!"

She smiled at him. "Great to see you too!"

Aevery laughed out loud. "And, Uncle Richard—how's that bowling hand?"

"They have a great league here," Richard said, beaming his beautiful smile.

Aevery shook everyone's hands and looked around again. "I don't see Cousin Franky? Where's he at?"

Carol stepped out of the crowd of relatives. She was holding a baby boy. "He's busy right now. He couldn't come, but he sends his greetings. And his love." She looked up at her grandson and caressed his cheek. "We've missed you so much, pumpkin! I want you to meet your grandfather." She gestured toward her husband. "This is Petty Officer 2nd Class, Paul Raymond Warrier."

Aevery vigorously shook his grandfather's hand. He couldn't hold back the tears as he hugged him for the first time. "It's great to finally meet you, sir. Thank you for your service and for your sacrifice."

As Paul squeezed his shoulder, Aevery hugged Carol and then took the hand of the baby. "Nana, you look so young!" The baby stared up into Aevery's eyes. "And who is this little one?"

Paul looked at him with a twinkle in his eye. "Aevery, this is your son."

Aevery couldn't help it. He bent over, hands on his knees, and cried. The memory of the frantic phone call from home flashed in his mind. The chills and dread he'd felt when he heard Candace's voice, choking back her tears, trying to be strong as she told him she had lost the baby. Once he was able to compose himself, he took the baby and kissed him. The baby touched his face.

"Son, you have to understand," Carol said, "sometimes miscarriages happen because the soul is not ready to come back. If there is no walk-in soul available, the baby can be lost."

Aevery wiped his tears away, hoisted the baby up in the air, and just looked at him. "What a beautiful boy. I was in country when I got the news. I felt so useless. I wasn't able to come home to be with Candace."

Carol comforted him. "You and Candace couldn't have done anything more, pumpkin."

"But that was ten years ago, Nana. Why is he still a baby?"

"He wanted to appear to you as a baby, because that's how you still think of him. And he wanted you to know that your baby is alive and well here."

A short distance away a young Marine in dress blue alphas caught Aevery's eye. He was just standing there, waiting his turn to greet his old friend.

"Oh my God! Is that you, Larson? Here, Nana, hold him for a sec—" Aevery handed the baby to Carol and ran to his friend. They hugged. Then he grabbed Cpl. Larson's hand and squeezed his shoulder. "You salty son-of-a-bitch! God, I've missed you!"

"So you did your twenty-two years!" Larson returned. "Congratulations, Gunnery Sergeant!"

"Wow! You look good. Last time I saw you—" the tears were flowing again "—you were in a body bag. I'm so sorry I sent you on patrol that night. That was such a hard decision—"

Larson interrupted him. "—But you had no

choice, Warrier. All the other Marines had families. You picked me because you trusted me to do my job. It was just my time. You know what we signed up for. 'The Few, The Proud.' Right?"

The two Marines smiled at each other, and Aevery chuckled through his tears. He looked back at Carol and Paul to make sure he hadn't imagined seeing them. His son was now a ten-year-old boy.

Larson brought him back to the conversation. "I was with you, you know? I was at every one of your Promotion Ceremonies." Larson could see his reflection in the unshed tears in Aevery's eyes. "One piece of advice, if I may, Warrier. Don't waste one day on guilt, it's a useless emotion. I lived a good life. I had good Marines like you to look up to."

"Thank you, Larson. That's much more than I deserve."

"Well, if you're able to work this out, you'll need to get some help."

Now Edward was standing beside Aevery as he said, "I can't work this out, Larson. I killed my—"

Edward interrupted him. "—We need to go, Aevery. Now."

Aevery turned to Edward. "What the hell? We just got here!" But when he looked back again to see his family, they were all gone. "Where'd everybody go?"

Edward reached out and shook Cpl. Larson's hand, "Good to see you again, Cpl. Larson. Please excuse us." Then he tugged at Aevery, who ducked away. So Edward grabbed him with one arm as if he were a sack of potatoes.

Surprised, Aevery shouted, "Whoa, man! I told you not to touch me!" He was still looking for his family.

Still holding the struggling Aevery a foot off the ground, Edward waved his other hand and they disappeared. In a split-second, they returned to the shore near the boat. The lantern on the boat was still the only light around.

Aevery was very upset as Edward pushed him toward the boat. "What the hell? I barely got to talk to anyone."

But Edward was not in the mood for games or explanations. "I have to get you back! Let's go!"

"Why do I need to get back? Back to what? I'm dead, remember?" But he reluctantly got aboard the boat.

Edward shoved off from the water, and once the boat was afloat, he suddenly appeared on the deck. He was relieved that Aevery had stopped resisting. "Thank you for cooperating," he said. "We need to hurry."

"I have nothing to get back to," Aevery repeated. He jumped overboard and started to wade back to the shore.

When Edward jumped over the side after him, he didn't land in the water. He flew over Aevery's head and touched down in front of him, then lifted him with both arms. They began wrestling.

Aevery struggled hard to get free, "Get your hands off me! I'm going back to Nana, Grandpa, my son and Larson!"

"No, you're not, you stubborn old mule! I'm taking you back."

Aevery stopped struggling. Convinced that he'd just had a change of heart and was ready to go quietly, Edward turned him loose.

Aevery turned to Edward and straightened his wet clothes. "You better watch your language there, son. That was a real zinger." He shook his head. "Stubborn old mule." He chuckled. "Amateur."

"What good is profanity?" Edward asked. "*You* are acting like a stubborn old mule. You think you always know what's best for you, even when you don't have all the information."

"I have all your information right here," Aevery said as he grabbed his own crotch. "I have nothing to go back to."

It was beginning to dawn on Edward that Aevery might not know the gravity of the situation. "Don't you understand?" he asked. "It was all an illusion!"

"Are you hearing yourself?" Aevery shouted back. "What the hell are you talking about?!"

"You're not really dead!" Edward shouted back.

"I shot a hole in my head! How could I not be dead?"

"Let me show you. Here, it'll save time." Edward reached for Aevery, who resisted, and they danced back and forth in the water as Edward kept trying to catch Aevery, who was finally successful at evading him.

"What?" the Marine shouted. "What are you doing? Don't touch me!" He started running in the shallow water, wildly splashing, bobbing and weaving back and forth.

Edward just stopped and held up his hands. Then he crouched down and slowly started to circle Aevery, not wanting to spook him. "Calm down! Easy, boy—" Edward clicked his tongue like he was calling a wild mustang.

"What the hell is that? What are you doing?"

"I'm not going to hurt you." Edward's voice was still calm and flat. "I just want to show you something. And we have to hurry," He disappeared, then reappeared again right behind Aevery and grabbed him.

"That's not even fucking fair!" Aevery shrieked. They began wrestling again.

Edward finally lost his patience. "I have to show you this!" He held Aevery's arms down with one hand and slapped his other hand against Aevery's third eye.

Aevery stopped struggling.

Chapter Eight

The Truth Is Exposed

Aevery was instantly transported back to his own bathroom on the night he'd committed suicide. But now he stood to one side and became an observer. It was all too familiar to him, as he knew what was going to happen, and he wasn't sure he wanted to see it. A sense of dread washed over him when he saw himself asleep in the bathtub, drunk, holding the bottle of bourbon in one hand, and his favorite 1911 pearl-handled revolver in the other. There was a prescription bottle of painkillers sitting on the side of the tub. He saw himself startle awake and sit bolt upright, pistol still in his hand. Then he saw himself take a swig, get a faraway look in his eyes, and then tear up.

He next heard himself say, "You lucky son-of-a-bitch, Larson. It's all over for you, your suffering's over." He saw himself take another swig and clear his throat. "You lucky bastard."

He saw himself look at his pistol. "I wish I had

the balls—"

As before, Candace knocked on the door. "Are you all right in there? You've been in there for *hours!*" she yelled. She tried the door, but it was locked. "Goddammit, Aevery, why do you have to lock the door?"

He heard himself yell at her. "For Christ sakes, Candace, I told you I just want to be left alone!" He watched himself wrestle with the bottle, pistol still in hand, get two pills out, swig them down, and clear his throat. He saw himself check the ammunition in the gun. He could see Candace through the door and the wall as she gave up, and went downstairs, grumbling under her breath. Then he saw Edward standing by, dressed again in his USMC World War I Dress Blue Delta uniform. But the Aevery in the bathtub couldn't see the angel. When a beam of light hit Edward, however, the Aevery in the bathtub saw the light. He thought his drunken mind was playing tricks on him.

Edward was listening as if he were on a phone call. "Yeah, I think he's getting ready to do it." He paused, and then listened again. "Are you sure you want me to leave him here like this?" He listened again. "Okay, I'll be right there." Edward disappeared.

Suddenly Aevery was transported to the heavenly courtroom of the Karmic Council. Again, he stood to one side and watched the scene as an observer. He looked up at the night sky ceiling and down at the cloud floor. Edward was standing before the Karmic Council of Seven Spiritual Beings. As Magda rose to her feet, Aevery muttered to himself, "Man, for an old lady, she sure is beautiful. Look at those eyes."

"You summoned me?" Edward asked her.

"Because of where we are in Earth's history," Magda said to Edward, "we have been given more leeway when it comes to suicides. We're going to allow you to intervene."

"Why now?"

Magda raised an eyebrow, "Because many human warriors are not fulfilling their Divine Purpose."

"It looks like Gunnery Sergeant Aevery Warrier will be the next—"

Magda raised her voice, interrupting him. "Help him! Teach him a lesson!"

Aevery paid close attention now. He was completely taken with Magda. "Oh, snap!" he thought.

A little exasperated, Edward looked at her. "Pardon me, Your Honor, but you didn't allow me to intervene last time. How do I—?"

"We *are* allowing it this time."

"Yes, Your Honor." Edward acquiesced, bowing his head, but still looking at her.

"If he is allowed to continue on this path," she explained, "it will become his Karmic Loop. The

Loop must be broken, Edward." All Seven Spirits stood in unison as Magda continued, "You have been afforded this opportunity. Now go and do what you will, as long as it harm none. And as long as his free will remains intact. Save him!"

"I just hope I'm not too late." With that, Edward disappeared.

Now Aevery was in his bathroom again, still observing what had happened on that fateful night.

Edward reappeared.

The Aevery in the bathtub, now very drunk, was raising the pistol. "I wish I could see him again," he slurred. "I'd tell him 'I'm sorry, so sorry you died, man.'"

Edward knew he had to act fast, so he raised a hand out of which shone a bright light.

Both Aeverys stared at the light. They spoke in unison, *"What the hell is that?"* The light spiraled, hypnotizing the Aevery in the bathtub, making him slowly sink back and pass out. His pistol-wielding hand went limp and hung over the side of the bathtub. The bottle of bourbon fell into the water.

This marked the end of what Edward wanted to show Aevery about that night.

Now Aevery again found himself wading in the shallow, dark surf of the Shining Isle.

Edward let him loose.

Aevery blinked a few times. "So you tricked me?

You tricked me, you son-of-a-bitch?"

Edward stood up resolutely and straightened his robes. "That's the lesson I came up with on such short notice. I've never done this before; they've never allowed me to intervene—"

A smile slowly grew over Aevery's face. "You sneaky devil, you."

Edward took offense and frowned but held his tongue.

Aevery ignored Edward's reaction. "So…you mean I'm not dead?"

"No, you're not dead."

Aevery jumped and raised his arms like a champion. "Yes! I'm not dead, I have another chance!" He hopped around and splashed Edward.

His patience growing even thinner, Edward said, "Hey! Listen!"

But Aevery paid no attention. He kept dancing around. "I'm still alive! I'm still alive—"

Edward grabbed Aevery again. And again, they wrestled until Edward finally shouted, "Listen to me! Calm down!"

"*Man*, you really are a downer, Eddie. You have to learn to loosen up." But now he was paying attention to the angel.

"In real time," Edward explained, "you're in a coma. I just got a message that we have to get your soul back to your body or you could really die."

"What? You mean that swirly light thing you did put me in a coma?"

"No, dingbat. It was your creative mixture of substances that put you in a coma."

"Ooooh! Dingbat." Aevery jumped on Edward's first-ever attempt at an insult. "Good one. A little wholesome, but still effective. That felt good didn't it?"

Edward had to smile. "Yeah it kinda did." Then he snapped back to the issue at hand. "Okay! Focus! All I did was hypnotize you so that I could create the illusion of your suicide." He straightened the boat in the shallow water.

Aevery finally realized the gravity of his situation, "Oh, crap! So we have to get me back? Can't you just wave your hand and get me back into my body?"

Edward stopped and looked straight at Aevery. "No, I can't. We actually traveled here, remember? Now we have to travel back We have to get you back to the Rainbow Bridge—"

"—Oh, great. I have to cross a gay bridge to get back to my body?"

Edward stopped pushing the boat and stared at Aevery. "You know, of course, that the gay community didn't adopt the rainbow flag until 1978. But the Rainbow Bridge has been in existence all throughout time. It's a part of Norse and Native American mythology. It connects the Spirit World to the Real World." He reached over and patted Aevery on the back. "You have your own personal bridge that connects your spirit to your body. You have to cross it, or your soul won't be able to return to your body. You'll die, or worse, you'll turn into a vegetable."

"What are we waiting for, then? Move your ass!" Sounding like a Drill Instructor, Aevery struggled to get back into the boat, and when he finally toppled in, Edward was already in the boat and dry. Aevery looked him up and down. "What the hell?" he gasped. "Why did you just let me struggle?"

"I couldn't help you, you didn't ask." Edward smiled down at him. "I thought maybe you *wanted to struggle* to get back in the boat."

"Yeah, sure. I just love to struggle when someone is standing right there who could help me."

Now Edward gave him a genuine smile. "I've been there your whole life, ready to help you, for what it's worth—" he took up the oar and began rowing, "—and never once did you heed a single sign I tried to give you."

Aevery just glared at Edward, not saying a word.

The further the boat went out into the sea, the darker it got. Strong winds blew, the white-capped waves made the boat rise and pitch.

"How did you get dry so quick?" Aevery finally asked.

"This is the spirit world, there is no such thing as wet or dry. You just think you should be wet, so you are."

"Then I want to be dry." Aevery looked down at himself, and he was now dry.

Another beam of light hit Edward. He rowed harder and faster. "We have to get you back to the Land of Night and Day."

Now Aevery couldn't help but notice the worried look on Edward's face. It gave him an unsettling feeling. The waves were big, and the boat was making no progress. "What's going on?" he asked. "What was that light thing?"

"Here, information and messages travel on beams of light. They just told me that you're in a bad way. We must get you back right away."

"Can't we go any faster?" Aevery asked, feeling desperate now. "It looks like we're not going anywhere."

The boat turned.

"Whoa!" Edward yelled. "I've never seen it like this."

"Like what? What, never?"

"You must really be resistant to going back."
Hearing that, Aevery threw a fit and began shouting. "What the hell? Why is everything my fucking fault?"

Thunder rumbled, and lightning struck all around them. Rain poured down. Edward stayed dry, but Aevery got soaking wet.

Edward shouted at Aevery through the pouring rain, "The sea was like glass on our way to the Shining Isle. We even had a tail wind because you wanted to go there, you couldn't wait to see your Nana and Grandpa."

Aevery lost his balance and fell flat on the deck. Edward was still lecturing. "Now you know that we're on our way back and you're scared. Calm down. It's all going to be okay. I'll be right there with you."

The boat struck a whirlpool and began spinning.

"Aevery, you must calm down."

"How can I calm down if we're in a hurry?" Aevery shouted back. "I'm dependent on you here. I've never been dependent on anyone for anything."

The sea became slightly calmer.

"There you go," Edward said in a soothing tone. "So, you don't like depending on people. Good, Aevery, good."

"Oh Jesus!" He didn't believe it, "And now you're going to psychoanalyze me? Dear God."

The boat turned into a wide channel.

"Just stating the facts," Edward said. "And I'm not Jesus or God."

"Where the hell are we going now?" Aevery asked.

"I know a shortcut. It's called the Dark Night Strait…it's kind of dangerous if you have loads of emotional baggage. But we'll get you back faster. Do you?"

"Do I what?" asked Aevery.

"Do you have loads of emotional baggage?"

"Are you hearing yourself? No! I'm a Marine, we

don't fucking have emotional fucking baggage. Let's go!"

Edward rowed harder, and the boat seemed to glide quickly into the Strait. The sky turned from black to dark red and filled with ominous clouds. Rain still poured down. Edward looked up into the clouds. "Oh, jeepers! Well, I thought this would be faster—"

"Jeepers? Did we just cross into the 1950s? What's the matter? What's wrong?" Aevery looked up as lightning struck inside the rolling clouds. The red sky cast a horrible light down on them. "Oh, God—that doesn't look good."

Edward had to set the record straight. "It looks like someone does have some emotional baggage."

"I do not!" But the sheepish, terrified look on Aevery's face told a different story. "Except for the nightmares. And the fact that I can't seem to connect to anyone. And the numbness. It's hard for me to feel…feel anything."

"Oh yeah? Well then, buckle up, Mister, we're in for one rough ride." Determination filled the angel. "Sometimes these things have to be faced. Head-on."

The boat slowed. Now the water looked thick.

Aevery leaned over the side. "The water looks weird. It looks red." He reached down and touched the thick, dark, water. When he pulled his hand back, he was horrified. "Oh Jesus Christ! It's blood! It's my nightmare!" He stood up as if he intended to run away, but his feet slipped on the wet deck. He fell onto his back and shuffled himself to the other side of the boat.

"This is you!" Edward shouted.

Aevery was too preoccupied with his surroundings to hear. He pointed to something in the water. "What is that floating over there?"

"Looks like a boot."

Aevery pulled himself to his knees and looked more closely. "It is a fucking boot!" When Edward, not surprised, nodded, Aevery looked around some more. "Oh my God! Look!" He pointed off the starboard side. "It's a Marine!"

As they came closer, an unconscious Marine floated by on a piece of car wreckage, one leg missing from his charred body. Smoke rising from the bloody water clouded Aevery's vision. He squinted and looked around in horror as more dead bodies of Marines rose to the surface, suddenly surrounding the boat.

When they heard a helicopter approaching, Edward looked up. There was a gleam of satisfaction in his eyes.

"Oh, dear God, no. No!" Aevery shouted. Edward stood back and watched as Aevery hit the deck, face down and covered his head, screaming, "Get down!"

The helicopter hovered overhead. Its light searched the boat. Edward sat calmly next to Aevery as bullets showered the boat.

"I can't do this! I can't keep having this nightmare! Not again, goddammit!"

Edward calmly lay on the deck beside his passenger, face down, and shouted over the noise of the helicopter, "Aevery, you can get out of this whenever you want to."

Aevery was trembling, panicked, wild-eyed. "I can't go home! Not until I'm in a body bag!"

There was still a glimmer of satisfaction in Edward's eye.

Aevery was slipping further away. "This war, what the hell is it all for? All the people lost…what for?"

Realizing he had to do something rash, Edward decided to join Aevery in his nightmare. Suddenly he was drenched. *"Look at me!"* He pushed Aevery onto his side to face him, but the Marine rolled over onto his back and kept looking around, frightened.

The helicopter still circled above, still searching the boat. Edward grabbed Aevery's head. "Look at me, you son-of-a-bitch! He grabbed Aevery by the jaw. "This is on you, snap out of it! It's me, Edward, I'm here with you. You're the only one who can get us out of here."

Aevery was still staring as the helicopter faded into the mist, but now the rapids turned into violent white water that tossed the boat up and down. The rain still poured on them, and now a huge wave crashed over them. It looked hopeless. Edward was really beginning to worry when the boat finally capsized. Just then a wide beam of light shot out of the water and up into the sky.

Chapter Nine

A Bridge in Need of Repair

A huge sandy mound lay on the beach beside a placid river. The sun shone bright, and seagulls called to each other. Edward and Aevery lay spooned together, Aevery in front and inside the mound. He opened his eyes and looked at the shadowy cocoon around them. The feathery pattern on the walls looked familiar to him, but he couldn't imagine why…or where he could be. Then he sensed someone with him, and knew it was Edward's chin on his shoulder. He finally spoke out loud. "You mind telling me what's going on here?"

It was an awkward situation. Edward cleared his throat. "I had to do…do…what I thought was necessary." He plucked a large white feather out of Aevery's hair.

Aevery clamped his eyes shut. "Don't touch me." He felt something touch his back. He opened his eyes. "That better be your chicken wing in my back!"

"No no no," Edward crooned. "I'm just happy to see you."

"Oh—my—God!" Aevery started struggling.

Edward merely rolled his eyes. "Angels don't have genitalia, genius." He opened his huge, impressive wings from around Aevery. They were the cocoon.

Aevery had large white feathers in his hair. The sudden, bright sunlight made him groan. As he sat up, he saw they were on the sandy riverbank and there was debris and pieces of the boat everywhere. "What the—? The last thing I remember was a helicopter circling us. And something about a son-of-a-bitch?"

"Yeah, you wigged out—flipped your lid—"

"I get it," Aevery snapped.

Edward shook like a dog. Sand flew all over Aevery. "Jesus!"

"Still not Jesus." Edward stretched out his wings and cracked his back to get the kinks out.

Aevery was starting to remember, "You called me a son-of-a-bitch, didn't you."

Edward straightened his robe and stood resolute. "Sorry I had to curse. I usually don't engage in such vulgarities."

Aevery smiled.

"That wasn't one of my shinier moments," the Guardian Angel continued. "I meant no disrespect to your mother. I thought if I joined you in your living hell, then you would snap out it." He paused.

"I was wrong."

"You're finally loosening up."

"I suppose I might be."

"I guess I need to thank you," Aevery said after a minute. "I think it did help for you to join me. I feel like now you know what I go through every time I try to go to sleep."

"I do know what you go through. And what you went through. I was there, remember? How do you think you survived?"

Aevery thought for a moment. "But if everyone has a Guardian Angel, why are there so many deaths?"

"It was in your contract to survive."

"What contract?"

"Every human signs a contract before reincarnating," Edward told him. "You agree to certain lessons. You were hell-bent, so to speak, on being a warrior again."

Aevery was still confused.

"Your committing suicide would've been a violation of your contract. It isn't always, but in your case, it would have been."

Aevery finally nodded. "Okay. I think I understand. I guess. Thanks for saving me. Both times."

"Well, now, that's a fine switch from 'Don't touch me!'" Edward did his best impression of Aevery and then laughed.

Aevery laughed, too.

"Let's get going," Edward said. "We have to continue on foot."

They stood up and began walking into the desert brush.

Hours later, they were still walking. At least, to Aevery, it seemed like endless hours of walking, they were now on a craggy path to steep cliffs that looked as huge as the Grand Canyon.

"How much longer till we get there?"

Edward looked at him, "When you no longer want to suffer, then we'll be there."

"So you're saying when I want to be there, we'll be there?"

"Precisely. You catch on quick." Edward pointed at the pile of rubble that was the not-quite-completed Rainbow Bridge. Its colors were dull and faded. "Here we are."

"Bullshit. This should be called the Land of the Never-Ending Mind Games."

Edward, sad and dismayed, surveyed the condition of the bridge."

"What?" Aevery asked, sounding exasperated, "what's wrong now?"

Edward pointed again. "Well—look at your bridge, it's not complete."

"Well, there may be another way to cross." Aevery moved to the edge of the canyon and looked down into the abyss below the bridge. He couldn't see the bottom. "Nah, that's pretty deep. There's no way I'm getting across there without the bridge. So…why is the gay bridge not complete?"

"This side," Edward explained, "is your shadow side, which all humans have. And in your case, we've seen that it's one rough ride." He pointed to the other side. "The other side is the love you have in your heart, which every human has." Then he pointed down into the abyss. "That's what keeps you from being able to embrace the love that's in your heart."

Aevery was staring down again.

"The Rainbow Bridge balances the two sides," Edward continued, "but apparently you aren't ready to embrace love. You haven't learned enough." He looked defeated. "It's a done deal. You can't go back."

"Dammit! I am, too, ready to go back!" Aevery stomped his foot, but he was standing too close to the edge. The canyon wall gave way and he began sliding down. Edward managed to catch him by one arm. Hanging there, Aevery wanted to close his eyes, but he couldn't stop searching for the bottom.

"This is all an illusion," Edward shouted. "You can do this, but if you let go and fall, you'll never get back to your body and you'll be lost in your misery forever."

Aevery, panicking now, looked down again.

"Don't look down!"

Aevery forced himself to look up at Edward. "How do I know I won't screw things up again?

How do I know my family isn't better off without me?"

"You have to have faith," Edward told him. "Trust that you are meant to be alive at this time. Trust!"

But Aevery looked disheartened. After a minute, his grip on Edward loosened, but Edward held on tighter. Then the angel adopted his Drill Instructor persona and barked at Aevery, "Your ancestors walked this road ahead of you. They made a place so you could be in this life right now." He reached down with his other hand to grab Aevery's shirt. "Are you gonna let fear and doubt rob you of that, ass-clown?"

Startled, Aevery looked down one more time, then mustered the strength to pull himself back up.

"I just don't think you're ready to go back." Edward looked very sad.

Aevery, angry again, grabbed him by the front of his robe. Both of them were surprised that he was able to hold on. Aevery was pleased and surprised for a second, but then he snapped back to angry and grappled Edward even harder. Edward chuckled a little.

"Yes! I am ready to go back. I miss my family. What will my wife and kids do without me? Sean and Becka need me. Candace and I were just getting to the point where we could start enjoying life. God, I have a lot of making up to do." He was not so intense now and loosened his grip on Edward. "And my brother. And my mom. She can't handle another death from war." He dropped to his knees, defeated. "Please, Edward. I want to go back. Please, I'm begging you." He grabbed onto Edward's robe again. "You've got to make this happen! Please!"

Edward looked over at the now completed Rainbow Bridge. Its bright and shiny colors glistened and twinkled.

Aevery looked, too. "Well, I'll be a son-of-a—"

Edward helped him up and shook his hand. "You did it, Mister. You made it." Edward beamed with pride. "Get going now, Marine. Cross your bridge."

Aevery blinked back tears, but he didn't move.

"Go on, cross now!" Edward pushed him toward the bridge.

As he stepped cautiously on the bridge, he looked back at Edward, who waved his hands in a shooing gesture. "Get going! Your time is almost up."

Aevery straightened up, adjusted his clothes, and walked halfway across the bridge. There he faltered, stopped, and looked back, unable to hold back the tears. He saw Edward standing with a myriad of angels behind him, also some beings without wings.

"Don't forget us angels and guides!" Edward shouted. "We're here to help you. But you have to ask!"

Aevery nodded, turned, and crossed to the other

side of the bridge.

Chapter Ten

A Rude Awakening

Aevery was engulfed in the familiar darkness. His consciousness wavered, but now he could hear a siren way off in the distance, also an engine drone and medical equipment. The voice of a young man echoed in his head: "Unit three-fifty-four, enroute to Stafford ER with forty-three-year-old male found unresponsive in the bathtub with alcohol and an unknown number of Vicodin nearby."

As two paramedics wheeled the unconscious Aevery into the Emergency Department, a nurse rushed in. A tearful Candace was running by his side. Edward was there, too.

The nurse looked at Candace. "You'll have to wait in the waiting room, Ma'am."

"We gave him ten units epinephrine, one to one hundred," the paramedic said to the nurse.

Another nurse hooked Aevery's blood pressure cuff to the hospital's equipment, pressed a button. It started to inflate.

Hours later, Candace was still sitting in the waiting room. A doctor walked up to her. "Mrs. Warrier, I'm Doctor Metzger."

"Yes?" Candace said anxiously, wiping a tear from her cheek.

"You can go in and see him now. He's stable."

Candace walked into Aevery's room. He was hooked up to what looked like countless machines. She sat down beside his bed and took his hand.

Edward, though she couldn't see him, was standing near the head of the bed.

"Hey," she said to her husband, "I know you probably can't hear me, but I really hope you pull through this." She started to cry again. "You know the kids would be devastated if something happened to you. I—I would be, too—" She kissed his hand and started to sob.

Edward bent down to whisper in Aevery's ear. "Aevery, wake up. Wake up."

Candace continued, still crying. "Who am I kidding? I just don't know how to help you anymore. I feel like I'm dying inside."

Aevery stirred and groaned, "Edward, help me, help me!"

Candace looked at him, then around the room. "Edward? Who is Edward?"

Edward held one hand over Aevery's solar plexus, which made it glow. "Aevery, tell her not to give up on you."

Aevery stirred a little more and moaned, "Candace, please don't give up on me." As she continued sobbing, he opened his eyes to a squint, groaned, and looked at her.

"Tell her you'll change," Edward advised.

Aevery managed to nod. "Please, Candace, don't give up on me. I swear I'll change. You'll see."

She smiled a little and wiped at her tears, "Okay, okay. Shhhh." She caressed his hair.

He moved in the bed and groaned. "Oh, God. My head—" He squeezed Candace's hand. "Promise me—you won't give up on me."

"It's all gonna be okay," she reassured him. "Sleep, Aevery."

The next day, in a private hospital room now, Aevery lay on his side in the bed. Edward stood nearby. Aevery opened his eyes and focused in on a foot-high ceramic figurine of an angel. Startled, he swung at it, nearly knocking it off his bedside table. "Don't touch me!"

A nurse named Violet happened to be standing there. She caught the figurine. "Careful!"

"Where did that come from?" he asked her.

She was still holding the figurine. "I don't know. It wasn't here before. It's beautiful, though." She set it down and opened the drawer of his bedside table. "They found this on you." She pulled out a large white feather and gave it to him. "Beautiful feather.

Very unusual. What kind of a bird feather is that?"

Aevery took the feather and smiled. "A cuckoo bird, I think."

She made a face at him and chuckled.

Edward flipped him off.

As Aevery looked at the feather, Violet walked around the bed and opened the curtains. As light blasted in, Aevery cringed and groaned. "Oh, dear God." He shielded his eyes with his hands.

"Breakfast will be here soon," the nurse said.

He was looking around the room now. "What happened, how did I get here?"

"You'll have to talk to the doctor when she arrives," Violet said. "All I can say is your Guardian Angel must've been working overtime."

Edward rolled his eyes. "You have no idea."

As the nurse started to leave, Aevery called out to her, "Hey, nurse? Can you ask the doctor to check my cholesterol?"

She nodded and walked out the door.

That evening, Candace returned to sit at her husband's bedside. He woke up from a long nap and took her hand. "Thanks for coming to visit me, Baby."

She bristled at his touch. "Baby? You haven't called me that in years. Your dinner tray is here." She stood up and rearranged things on his bedside table.

Aevery sat up. "I'm sorry about that. I know I

probably don't have the right to call you Baby anymore."

She looked closely at him. "What's gotten into you?"

Edward was still there, still listening.

"Oh, I get it," Candace was saying. "You just want to butter me up." She nodded as if she knew what he was up to.

"No," he protested, "I'm not trying to butter you up, I'm serious." He took a sip of tea. "I've been through something, and—well, I want to change." He turned his head and spoke under his breath. "Edward, help me out here." He cleared his throat.

She looked at him, obviously not believing him. "Okay. Whatever." She turned to pick up his water pitcher, but he grabbed her hand and pulled her toward him and into a hug. "Let me stop you right there," she said. "Aevery," she added in a flat voice. "I've consulted with a lawyer about a divorce."

Light shot out from Edward's hand, and Aevery's solar plexus began to glow.

Aevery was shocked, but he couldn't blame her. "I've been a real asshole," he said. "Thank you for being there for me through thick and thin, through all my deployments, even when I didn't deserve it. I couldn't ask for a better wife. I love you and the kids. I'm gonna prove it to you."

Candace blinked back more tears. "I—I don't know what to say."

Aevery was resolute in his sincerity, "There's

nothing to say. Just stand back and watch me. If you want a divorce, I'll give you one, but I'll never stop trying to get you back."

As she burst into tears again, he pushed his bedside table away and pulled her into a hug. She sobbed into his chest.

Edward smiled and nodded.

Later, as they sat and ate dinner together, Aevery took a sip of tea and almost choked, as if he'd suddenly remembered something. "Can you do me a big favor?"

"Sure." She took a bite of her meat.

"Would you take Grandpa's diamond cufflinks to the bank and put them in the safe deposit box?"

"Why?" she asked as she chewed.

"You know," he told her, "I may say weird stuff, or ask you to do some strange things, but just bear with me, okay?" He wiped his mouth and pushed the bedside table away. "That hospital food isn't bad." He took her hand and kissed it.

Aevery was sitting in an Alcoholics Anonymous meeting. "My name is Aevery Warrier, and I'm an alcoholic."

Everyone attending the meeting said in unison, "Hi, Aevery."

Aevery and Becka sat on the sofa, watching a movie together. They were enjoying popcorn.

"You know what, Becka-Lou? I was thinking we could play racquetball like we used to…years ago." The memory of teaching his eight-year-old daughter how to play racquetball was a memory he'd long cherished. The memories of all the times they played, her getting better and better as the years went by had been his go-to memory when he was deployed to Iraq. But when he returned home from one of those deployments, she had found boys and was no longer interested in playing racquetball with her old man. Now Aevery was a little apprehensive to even broach the subject with her.

But Becka smiled at him. "All right. But you may walk away embarrassed. I've been playing at school.

"Oh ho ho! Is that a challenge?" he asked, smiling from ear to ear.

"Yes, it is. I've got skillz, Dad." She brushed off her shoulder.

Aevery nodded and smiled.

Aevery and Becka were playing their first game of racquetball, both of them drenched with sweat, red-faced, and breathing hard. Aevery hit the ball, it hit the wall, and bounced pretty far back. Becka slammed the ball against the back wall, and it flew all the way to the front wall.

"Nice shot, Becka-Lou!" He dived for the ball, but it flew past him.

"Thirteen-five," she announced, smiled, and brushed off her shoulder again.

Aevery laughed. "I gotta admit, you're good."

When the game was finished, they walked out of the court. Aevery was still out of breath and drenched with sweat.

She wiped her face with a towel. "Good game, Daddio."

"Yes, it was, Pumpkin." He took a deep breath.

Candace had known for years that her son was gay. She was pleased now that Aevery seemed to know, too, and was accepting of it. The family had dinner with Sean and Jake one night. Candace had told Sean before the dinner that his father knew and was accepting. Sean felt liberated to be able to sit next to his boyfriend and not have to pretend they weren't a couple. Sean touched Jake's leg under the table. Jake smiled at him. The family laughed, talked, and enjoyed their dinner.

Life was finally getting back to normal. Not normal as in before "the suicide," but normal in the way things had been years before when the family had been close. Aevery, Candace and Becka went out for coffee one afternoon.

As they walked out of the shop carrying their coffees, a lady was walking in with her five-year-old son. The boy pointed and laughed at Becka, "Mommy look at the fat lady."

Candace looked surprised and frowned. As she looked at Becka to gauge her reaction, Avery crouched down in front of the boy. "It's not okay to talk about people's bodies—ever."

The boy looked a little scared as his mother said, "Hey—don't talk to my son like that!"

Aevery stood up straight and looked the boy's mother in the eye. "Maybe you should teach your kid some manners." He pointed at Becka. "That's my daughter, and I don't appreciate anyone insulting her."

The boy's mother, insulted herself, grabbed her son by the arm and pulled him back out the door.

Aevery smiled as she stomped away and called after her, "Have a great day!"

Candace and Becka could only stare at him in awe.

"What?" he asked. "It's true, that little fucker needs to learn some manners." He took a casual sip of his coffee.

Candace and Becka looked at each other and smiled.

Chapter Eleven

A Thief at the Dinner Table

Aevery was now comfortable with the progress he had made with his immediate family, so he figured it was time to start working on his brother. He dreaded it, but he knew it had to be done. He had abandoned Tony, twice, and needed to make amends. He decided he would start by inviting him to a family dinner at their house.

Sean, Jake, Becka, and Tony were sitting at the dining room table. Tony sat next to Becka, across from Sean and Jake. The table was beautifully set with Candace's finest china and silverware. Aevery and Candace began to bring in the dishes of food. A large serving tray beautifully displayed a perfectly cooked roast with carrots and cabbage around it. Other platters held mashed potatoes, gravy, dinner rolls with butter, and a green salad.

"Tony, I'm really glad you could make it," Aevery said as he sat down and unfolded his cloth napkin.

Tony gave his brother a straight-faced look of false gratitude. "Yeah. What a privilege to be invited to big brother's house for dinner."

The tension was thick. Everyone looked around awkwardly. Becka gave Sean a sharp look as she spooned some mashed potatoes onto her plate.

Candace chuckled and said, "Well, I hope I didn't overcook the meat."

Aevery winked at her. "Everything looks perfect, Sweetheart."

The room was silent, except for the tapping of forks and knives on the plates. The food was passed around, and everyone began eating. Dinner conversation was forced. The topics of weather, local sports teams, and the goings-on at Becka's high school were completely worn out by the time dinner ended.

Tony acted like an uninvited guest and spoke only when spoken to.

Finally, Aevery wiped his mouth for the last time. "Wow, what a delicious meal, Candace."

"Yes," Tony said, "delicious dinner, Candace. Thank you. Really."

Candace stood up. "Don't anyone go anywhere," she said in a bright voice. "I have dessert and coffee. Strawberry cheesecake."

Tony sighed, "Oh, wow, I'm stuffed. Maybe later?"

Aevery stood up, too. "I have an appointment upstairs; I'll be right back." He excused himself and went upstairs to use the toilet.

While he was gone, Tony sat quietly for a bit, fidgeting with his napkin. Finally, he said, "Uh—I need to talk to Aevery in private. I'll be right back." He excused himself and hurried up the stairs.

Aevery was washing his hands in the master bathroom. He looked in the mirror. "Edward, you've got to help me with Tony. I've got to get through to him somehow."

Edward nodded.

Aevery walked out of the bathroom to find Tony poking around in Candace's jewelry box.

When he glimpsed Aevery, he slammed the lid shut and turned around. "I—I was just—"

"—looking for Grandpa's diamond cuff links?"

"What?" Tony chuckled nervously. "No!"

Aevery slowly moved toward his brother. "Then what would you be doing in *my wife's* jewelry box?"

Tony clumsily started to move around Aevery, but Aevery grabbed him by the collar. "I wasn't after any such thing!" Tony nearly shouted.

But Aevery knew better. "Oh, yes, I know you'd love to pawn those diamonds. But they're going to my son someday."

"You don't know me, man," Tony shot back. "Ever since you went into the Marine Corps, you think you're above everybody. Well I've got news for you, jackass," he ripped Aevery's hands away from his collar and pushed him in the chest. "You're just as much an alcoholic and addict as I am. You're not any better than anyone else!"

Aevery glared at him. They were both ready to fight.

"And," Tony smirked, "what would that *faggot* son of yours need with diamond cuff links, anyway?"

Aevery punched him right in the mouth, then grabbed him by the shoulders and shook him. "My son is *three times the man* you'll ever be, you drug-addled son-of-a-bitch!"

Tony wiped the blood from his mouth, straightened himself up, and adjusted his clothes. "You have no idea what you put Mom through. I got so tired of hearing her cry herself to sleep every night after you enlisted. I had no other choice than to go away."

"Oh yeah, you did," Aevery said, "you had plenty of other choices."

"Oh yeah? Like what?" Tony seemed confident that Aevery wouldn't have anything worthwhile to tell him.

"Like making something of yourself."

Tony laughed, "Yeah, sure. I could've enlisted like you did. And really broke Mom's heart."

Aevery shook his head, "No, I get it, the military wasn't for you. But you could've gone to college and made something out of yourself." He stepped closer to his brother. "My only mistake was enlisting when I did, instead of waiting until you graduated from high school. I should've made sure you had a plan. That was, what? Four or five years of your life? I'll take the blame for that," he pointed at Tony, "but you—you've made bad choices for well over twenty years."

Tony raised his arm, his hand already curled in a fist.

Edward immediately sent light to Aevery's solar plexus. It began to glow, and in that instant, Aevery remembered how Tony had cried when he'd hugged their mother goodbye back in 1991 when he was leaving for boot camp. He remembered how he mussed Tony's hair on the way out the door. Then his memory reached back in time to an earlier life when his Native American brother Tony had cried over his dead body after he'd jumped from the cliff. Then he saw the light from the bivouac fire flickering on his brother's face as he tried to warn him about their father's disapproval during the Civil War. He shook off the memories, sighed, and stepped back.

"Why don't you get your life together?" he asked in a quieter voice. "You're still young. You can make something of yourself. I'll even help you."

"Yeah, sure you'll help me."

"I'm dead serious. Come to AA meetings with me. Let's go to some meetings together. Let's get clean and sober. Together."

Tony stance and voice both revealed his life-long skepticism. "What makes you think I need your fucking help?"

"Oh, I don't know—maybe because you're thirty-seven, and you've got nothing to show for your life. No wife, no kids. You're still living with roommates and working part-time. Barely making it."

Tony lunged at Aevery, trying to get him in a headlock. They began to wrestle.

"The truth hurts, doesn't it?" Finally tired of Tony's shenanigans, Aevery threw him to the floor like a rag doll. "We're done here," he snarled. "You're not gonna put your fucking hands on me in my own home." He picked Tony up off the floor. "That's right, Tony. This is my home!" He pushed him out the bedroom door.

The rest of the family had gathered in the living room, when they heard the yelling start, just in time to see Tony angrily stomp down the stairs, Aevery right on his heels.

"And don't you ever try to steal something from me again!" Aevery was shouting. "You will never get your hands on those cuff links. They're mine!"

By the time the family reached the foot of the stairs, Tony was storming out of the house. Aevery and the family followed. When Tony got into his rattletrap car, wiping the blood off his mouth, Aevery shouted after him, "I meant what I said about helping you! If you want my help, come to the AA Club!"

Tony flipped him off as he backed out of the

driveway. Aevery laughed and started to walk toward the front door.

Candace looked at Aevery. "How did you know he would try to steal your cuff links?"

Aevery nodded and smirked, "Let's just say a big, awkward bird told me."

Chapter Twelve

Revelations over Cocoa

Aevery knocked on the door of his mother's apartment, regretting that he had let his erroneous perceptions color his feelings for the woman who had given him life. Inside, Janice, who was reading, jumped up to look out the window. She gasped to see her son standing there. When she opened the door, the two stood motionless for a long moment, just looking at each other. Although neither of them could see him, Edward stood behind Aevery, watching their interactions.

Finally, Janice broke the silence, "Son, this is a surprise!" She motioned for him to enter. "Come in!"

Feeling he finally understood his mother like never before, Aevery kissed her on the cheek and walked through the door. Edward came in too.

Janice felt odd and caught off guard. *What could he possibly want?* she wondered, though she forced herself to be cordial. "Have a seat, son. Can I get you something to drink?"

"Well…since you offered, I have been hankering for some of your hot chocolate, like when we were kids."

"I don't know if I have all the ingredients, but I can check." Janice went into the kitchen. All of a sudden, she felt nervous and ill at ease. She couldn't stand it anymore, so she decided to speak up and called to him, "So what brings you all the way from Virginia, Son? And without calling, so I could clean and get some groceries?" She rustled around in the kitchen cupboards.

Aevery came in and sat at the kitchen table. "I didn't want to put you out. Actually, I wanted to talk to you about something," he admitted, "and you may just be the only person who will believe me and understand."

She put the kettle on to boil and sat down at the kitchen table across from him. "Well, now you've piqued my interest." She felt a little more at ease. "But why do you think *I'll* believe you and understand?"

"I know I've given you a hard time about your *weird* spiritual beliefs before…" he began, not thinking about his choice of words.

"Weird?" she said a tad defensively, chuckling awkwardly.

He backpedaled just slightly. "Well, they were weird to me at the time. You have to realize, Mom, that a Marine can't rely on anyone but himself. But, well, I've had a—" he couldn't believe what he was about to say, "—a spiritual experience."

"Really?" she asked, eyes wide.

"Well…"

"Don't worry, son, you can tell me anything."

It was hard for him to admit to what he knew was his weakest moment, "Mom, a while back, I was in a bad way." He spoke carefully, gauging her reaction. "I was suicidal and came damn close to killing myself."

"Oh, God. Son, I'm sorry." Her concerned eyes searched his face for answers, "What happened?"

His tone lightened, and he smiled. "My—my Guardian Angel saved me."

As Janice studied her son's face, she smiled. "Guardian Angel? Wow!"

Edward was looking proud.

"He tricked me into thinking I had killed myself."

Janice gasped.

"He showed me what would happen if I had really done it." He pointed toward her living room, "Edward and I were standing right over there when Candace called you to tell you."

Janice's eyes filled with tears. "Edward?" she asked.

"That's the angel's name. He's probably standing right here. Or close by," Aevery said matter-of-factly. "Apparently he accompanies me wherever I go."

His mother nodded. "Yes, that would be a Guardian Angel's job."

"See, that's why I wanted to come here. I knew you'd get it. You'd know what I'm talking about. Anyway, you cried when Candace called you."

Janice gently took Aevery's hand, "Of course I would cry. You're my son, we may have had our differences…but—"

"—I saw my autopsy, my cremation, my memorial. And then the most interesting part…"

Janice was dumbfounded at hearing her son talk this way. "That must've been hard to see," she said quietly. "Then what?" She got up and brought two cups, spoons, and a few canisters to the table.

"He took me back to past lives. Mine and the kids." He watched as she spooned the chocolatey mixture into the cups. "Then he took me to the Shining Isle to see the family. I saw Nana and finally got to meet Grandpa."

"Oh, really?" She kept her tone nonchalant. "How are Mom and Dad? It's been awhile since I've been there."

"You've been there??"

"Yes, several times. I go when I'm troubled or need answers."

"But how? How do you…?"

"You can get there through what they call journeying. Or by guided meditation."

"Well," he was searching for the best way to say

what he had to say, "well, Nana and Grandpa looked so young. And they had a baby with them."

"A baby?"

"It was my son, you know, the baby that Candace lost when I was deployed?"

Janice gasped, her hand to her mouth.

Aevery added. "Nana told me that miscarriages happen because the soul is not ready to come back, and if there's no walk-in soul, the baby is lost."

Janice looked surprised. "Fascinating!" She teared up and took Aevery's hands, "Wow, that sounds like it was quite an adventure, son."

Aevery teared up, too, but then chuckled, "I saw Aunt Hazel and Uncle Richard, too."

Janice chuckled through her tears, "How's Aunt Hazel?"

"She looked really good," he said. "And they were all a lot younger. It was really something, Mom."

"Sounds like it."

Aevery wasn't finished yet. "Edward also showed me a therapy session you had right after I retired. You were talking to your therapist about Grandpa's death."

She looked a little shocked, then looked up toward the ceiling. "Edward," she said in a stern voice, "therapy sessions are supposed to be confidential." Then she smiled.

Edward laughed, too, and then shot light at Aevery's solar plexus.

In that instant, Aevery was transported in his memory to his grandfather's funeral. He remembered how young Janice had cried as she consoled her mother. His memory then floated to when Janice broke down in tears during her therapy session. Next, he remembered the horrified look on Janice's face as Candace told her over the phone that he was dead. His voice echoed in his ears: *She doesn't care that much*. He shook off the memories and put his hand on his mom's. "I'm glad I got to see that. It helped me to understand where you're coming from."

Janice nodded and squeezed his hand.

"I got to see Grandpa's funeral, too," he added. "I'm sorry you had to go through that at such a young age, Mom." Janice looked flabbergasted, but he pushed ahead anyway. "So you were at my graduation, huh?"

Shocked, she teared up again. "I'm so sorry, son, that's one of my biggest regrets." Now she broke down and really cried. "If I could do it over, I'd run to you and congratulate you!"

"It's never too late, Mom," he said. They stood up together and hugged.

"Congratulations, son!" she squealed through her tears, "I'm so proud of you! I love you so much!" She began sobbing into his shoulder.

He was also crying and hugged her tightly. "I love you too, Mom."

Edward hugged them both.

Several minutes later, Aevery and Janice were still sitting at the kitchen table and drinking hot cocoa.

Aevery sniffed his cocoa, exhaled with pleasure, and sipped it carefully. "God, I've missed your cocoa. It tastes just the same as when we were kids."

"What is that…your third cup? I may just have to cut you off."

He swallowed. "I have some more news…I guess."

"Oh?" she said as the chocolatey steam rose from her mug. "There's more?"

"Sean is gay, Mom."

"Oh. Well, I had my suspicions."

"What?"

"Aevery," she said, taking another sip, "people notice those things. One of Nana's brothers was gay. Uncle Richard, you know?"

"Uncle Richard?" Aevery sounded surprised.

"But…but he was such a great bowler!"

"What does that have to do with anything?" Janice laughed. "Lots of athletes are gay."

"Well…it's just that…who would've thought?"

"No one in the family would talk about it," she said. "But we knew."

"Well," he admitted after a minute's thought, "I guess people notice those things when they're sober." He took another sip of cocoa to steady himself. "But finding out about Sean hit me like a ton of bricks." He shook his head and sipped again. Janice gave a casual nod. "All of us are glad Sean doesn't have to live in the closet like Uncle Richard did."

Aevery nodded.

"Oh, son," she said in a brighter tone, "I just remembered. I saw something and thought of you." She went to a shelf, picked up a glossy pamphlet, and brought it to him. "That organization does wonderful work with veterans. You should look into it. They have retreats."

Aevery set his mug down and looked at the pamphlet.

Chapter Thirteen

A Ball and a Bearskin Rug

Dressed in his Dress Blue Alphas for the first time in many years, Aevery was standing in a ballroom in Las Vegas. The heavy wool coat was hot, but he was proud to be one of the few who rated to wear it. This was the first Marine Corps Ball he and Candace had attended in many years. Toward the end of his career in the Corps, they had grown tired of going every year, but this year, with his new lease on life, it seemed appropriate for them to attend again. This time it would be a celebration. His numerous medals sparkled against the navy-blue of his coat, as Aevery walked, carrying two glasses, one filled with champagne, the other with orange juice, to their table where Candace was sitting. She was wearing a beautiful, sparkling, burgundy ball gown, and her hair was beautifully styled in an up-do, with sparkly pins strategically placed here and there.

He set her glass on the table in front of her, then

sat down and gestured with his glass for a toast. She raised her glass and smiled. "To my beautiful wife," he said as they clinked glasses and he wrapped his arm around hers. They both sipped from their glasses, then kissed. "May I have this dance?" As they danced, Aevery decided to share something else on his mind. "So, Mrs. Warrier—"

"—yes, husband of mine?"

"We have a special anniversary coming up."

Candace nodded.

"Twenty years." He grinned. "Whoa—how many Marines can say that?"

She chuckled, "Not many, I would presume."

"Well…I'd like to take you on a trip and do something special for our twentieth."

"Like what?" she asked, her curiosity piqued.

"Like, I want to surprise you."

"Well! How wonderful. I'm in!"

They laughed and continued to dance. He kissed her gently, "Mmm, your lips taste like champagne."

Just then, Staff Sgt. Johannas came walking up with his wife, Mandy. "We finally made it," he told them.

Aevery and Candace stopped dancing. "Better late than never, man."

Johannas shook Aevery's hand and hugged Candace. Aevery and Candace hugged Mandy, too.

Aevery pointed to their table. "We're right over there."

Weeks later in a remote, snow-covered, mountain lodge, Aevery led a blindfolded Candace up the stairs, and into the luxurious master suite. He took the blindfold off and she was amazed. A fire crackled in the fireplace, before which she saw the customary bearskin rug. Candles were lit around the room and there were rose petals all over the bed.

Candace gasped, "Oh, Aevery! This is so romantic." She wrapped her arms around him, and they kissed and kissed again. They kissed faster and more passionately and soon started undressing each other. As she ran her hands up under his sweater, he pulled her pants down. When she tried to step out of them, she fell over onto the bed, taking him with her. They were still lip-locked. As they fell onto the bed, the bedframe broke. She screamed, but they didn't miss a beat, rolling around and kissing, with some giggling in there too. They rolled right off the far side of the bed and thudded onto the floor. Even the fall didn't deter them. They rolled over onto the bearskin rug by the fire, both half dressed, and still kissing. Finally, they took a breath.

Aevery couldn't resist. "That is *exactly* how I had it planned."

Candace burst out laughing. It was a nice icebreaker, considering they hadn't had sex in well over three years. Aevery had been very nervous, afraid that his little guy wouldn't cooperate, but he'd finally psyched himself up by reassuring himself that sex isn't everything, and that whatever happened, it would be an intimate weekend with the woman he loved and who had supported him through their entire marriage. Shaking off his insecurities, he now moved in slowly and kissed her long and tender. She ran her hands through his hair. She sighed in his ear. This was the first time they had been intimate without some sort of alcohol in his system. Aevery was pleasantly surprised by the way his body was responding to his wife.

About an hour later, firelight flickered as Aevery and Candace sat in afterglow by the fireplace. The bed behind them was in shambles.

Candace looked at him, her eyes twinkling. "Wow, that was nice."

He smiled and looked proud, but inside he was mostly relieved. "I think it's time for a little bubbly." He reached over and pulled a bottle of sparkling cider out of the champagne bucket.

"Boy, you thought of everything, didn't you?"

"Yep. A good Marine is always prepared for anything." He picked up his pants nearby, rummaged through the pockets, found his keys, and used the bottle opener. "I got the really good stuff. It needs a bottle opener instead of a corkscrew." He poured two glasses and handed one to Candace. "To twenty years of marriage to the best wife any man or Marine could ever have." He raised his glass for a toast. As she teared up, he turned serious. "I love you," he whispered, his chin quivering. "Thank you for putting up with me, raising our kids, and keeping the home fires burning while I was out doing my thing."

Edward was now in the room with them. As he raised his hand and shot light to Aevery's belly, Aevery suddenly remembered standing before the tribe to be married to his lovely maiden, an earlier Candace. Then came the memory of knowing her in high school but being too shy to talk to her, and finally asking her out in his senior year. He remembered their tearful breakup when he told her of his decision to enlist in the Marine Corps. He remembered the crushed look in her eyes. Then he recalled his shot-in-the-dark phone call to her from Mogadishu, trying to rekindle their relationship. His mind sped forward to marrying her. He was dressed in his dress blue alphas, rank of corporal on his sleeves. His mind suddenly flipped to his Native American love who had just given birth to their son, but then the memory changed again, and Candace had just given birth to baby Sean. She handed him the baby, and as he looked at his newborn son, the baby's face flickered back and forth between his Native son, and baby Sean. The clink of their glasses brought him out of his memories.

"And I love you, Aevery. Happy Anniversary, baby," she said.

They kissed again.

Months later, Aevery sat in a therapy room at

the Veteran's Administration in a circle with other veterans. A veteran without legs was talking. Many of them were visibly uncomfortable.

A few weeks later, a group of veterans and their families were sitting together around a campfire at a wilderness retreat center. They were all attending a Retreat for Veterans with PTSD. They were sharing their stories of their traumas.

Candace was sitting at Aevery's side as he slowly shared one of his stories. "I met Larson in Basic. He was my best buddy. We managed to get into the same infantry units. I promoted faster than he did." He looked down, "We deployed to Iraq together. I hand-picked him to go with us. He was so fired up and ready." He nervously wiped his hands on his pants. "Then one night I sent him on patrol. It was one of the hardest decisions I've ever made." His voice cracked. "All the other Marines had families at home—and I knew he could handle it." He forced himself to finish his story. "Well…he was killed when their Humvee hit an IED."

Candace rubbed his back.

Chapter Fourteen

The Angel Feather

Aevery had begun attending Alcoholics Anonymous meetings right after he came home from the hospital. At times, he attended several meetings a week. He had gotten himself a sponsor and was doing well at staying clean and sober. This meeting seemed like any other meeting. But not quite. The table seemed a little more crowded than usual.

John, the leader, reached the chip-accepting part of the meeting, milestones in days of sobriety. "Is anyone accepting their one-month chip?"

When a woman raised her hand, she was given a chip, and the whole room applauded for her.

"Is anyone accepting their sixth month chip?" John asked.

Silence. Minutes later, a couple of people took chips for seven and ten months.

"One year?" John asked.

As Aevery raised his hand and smiled, applause broke out. He got up and went to accept his chip and came to sit back down. Seeing Tony standing in the doorway, he went over and shook his hand, then hugged him and coaxed him to come in and sit down. Several attendees shifted seats so Tony could sit by Aevery. A minute later, a woman came out of the kitchen with a cake and one lit candle. Aevery laughed.

Aevery stood in the rectory of a local church wearing his dress blue alphas, his white cover under his arm. He was alone except for Edward, and nervously pacing back and forth. He finally spoke. "Edward, I could really use your help right now. Help me say the right words."

As Edward gave him a thumbs up, Sean walked in, looking very handsome in a black tuxedo with a white shirt, black and blue paisley vest, matching tie, and pocket square, plus a pale blue boutonniere in his lapel. He wore diamond studs in both ears.

"Wow! Look at you!" Aevery exclaimed. "You clean up nice, don't you, son?"

As Sean chuckled a little, then sighed, Edward sent light to Aevery's belly with his raised hand. His solar plexus glowed. "Dad, I'm really nervous," Sean admitted. "Thank you for being here."

"I wouldn't miss your wedding for the world." Aevery couldn't help looking a little sheepish. "I'm sorry I wasn't there for you earlier when you needed me."

"Oh, Dad, please," Sean waved off his father's sentimentality. "I know it took you awhile to accept me being gay, but now, I'm just so happy that you understand."

Yes, he understood. But still, Aevery couldn't stop the memories from flooding back to him. The exhilarating feeling of finally finding a man who shared his feelings. Of kissing Bosen, and their moment of passion in the creek. Then the horror in Bosen's eyes when he was stabbed in the stomach. Aevery looked at his son and sighed, "I understand perfectly well."

Edward laughed out loud, though neither man heard him. "That's the understatement of the century!"

Aevery began to pat his pockets. "Son, I…I have something for you."

"Oh?"

Aevery produced a little black box.

"Oh my God, Dad, what is this?"

Aevery opened the box. "These were your great grandfather's diamond cuff links. He wore them when he married Nana, and I've worn them on many special occasions, including the day you were baptized. And now I want you to have them."

Sean teared up. "Wow, Dad!"

Aevery took the cuff links out of the box. The huge diamonds glistened brightly. Sean removed his silver cuff links and stood quietly as his father inserted the diamonds.

"They're beautiful! And they match my earrings. Thanks, Dad."

They hugged. Edward joined in.

"I love you, son. Congratulations. I'm so glad you found someone to love."

Later, in the sanctuary, Aevery and Candace sat in the front pew and watched as Sean and Jake were married. Becka, wearing a beautiful blue gown. served as an honor attendant. Aevery looked adoringly at his tearful wife and squeezed her hand, then turned and smiled at the two grooms' grandmothers sitting right behind them.

A few years passed. Now the family was gathering to see Becka graduate from George Mason University with her bachelor's degree. Aevery, Candace, and Sean posed for pictures with her dressed in her cap and gown, decorated with gold braided cords that showed she was graduating with honors. As Jake took the pictures, they all hugged and congratulated her.

A year or so later, in a beautifully decorated reception hall, Becka and her husband Charlie cut their wedding cake. The groom fed the bride a piece of the cake, and she smiled and laughed.

As Aevery looked on, the memory of Becka's past life from 1932 flashed through his mind.

Becky took a bite of soda cracker, "You know what, Momma?"

"What, angel?"

"When we get money again, I want to have cake every day."

Then little Becky morphed into four-year-old Becka. She blew out the big candle and looked up adoringly at her father.

Aevery got up from the table. "Would you like me to get you a piece of cake, baby?" he asked Candace.

"I would love one. Thank you."

Aevery walked toward the cake table.

Later on, Aevery and Becka danced the father/daughter dance. As usual, Edward was standing off to one side.

"I'm so happy for you and Charlie," Aevery was saying. "Such a great guy for you, Becka-Lou."

"He certainly is, Daddio."

"And I'm so proud of you, too. You knew just what you wanted, and you went after it. Just like a Warrier!" They laughed together.

"Thanks," she said. "It's so good to have the whole family here. Especially you, Dad. I don't know what I would've done without you in my life. So many of my friends' parents are divorced and some of them don't have the best relationships with their Dads." She teared up. "I'm so glad you're home."

"Well, thanks Becka-Lou. But I had help."

Edward smiled, looking proud again, as Becka kissed her dad on the cheek and they hugged.

Ten years later, Aevery was reading a book to his grandchildren, four-year-old Brittany, five-year-old Brock, and Jessica, age eight. The book had a huge angel on the cover. Aevery was holding his white feather. He looked into the faces of each child. "And what does Grandad always say?" he asked.

The children answered in unison. "Angels can only help us if we ask!"

"That's right. High five!" He high fived each child with Edward's feather. The Angel figurine from the hospital sat on the mantle above where they were all sitting.

"Is that really an angel feather, Grandad?" Jessica searched his face for any signs that he was teasing them.

"Cross my heart," Aevery said, crossing his heart with the feather. "Here. You want to see it again?" He held out the feather.

Wide-eyed and awestruck, she carefully took it from him.

Just then, Sean and Jake walked in from the kitchen, followed by Becka and Charlie coming in to round up their kids, too.

"Come on, Jess," Sean said. "It's time to go. Tell Grandad goodbye."

Jessica frowned. "Awwww, do I have to?"

Aevery squatted down to her eye-level and looked seriously at her. "You've got to do what your dad tells you. Next time you come over, you can play with the feather."

They both laughed, and Jessica leaned in close to her grandad's ear. "I'm gonna ask my angels to make my daddies let me stay longer next time." Everyone laughed.

Twenty years later found Aevery and Candace both in their seventies. Their fiftieth wedding anniversary celebration was in full swing with the whole family present, even Edward, as usual standing silently nearby. Jessica, now twenty-eight and very pregnant, toasted her grandparents.

Standing next to Aevery, Candace, and a huge cake, she lifted her champagne glass full of sparkling cider and began to speak. "I just wanted to say congratulations to the two most important people in my life, besides my dads and my husband." She wiped a tear away. "I don't know what I would've done without you while I was growing up. Your marriage has been a safe harbor to all of us." She looked down at her glass as she continued. "Carl and I want a marriage just like yours. May all of our marriages turn out to be as successful as yours!"

Glasses clinked all around the room. Aevery and Candace kissed, and then interlocked their arms to share sips of sparkling cider. Suddenly the crowd gasped. Aevery looked up. Jessica was grabbing at her stomach, obviously in pain.

The immediate family next gathered in the maternity ward's waiting room at Stafford Hospital. Sean and Jake, now in their mid-fifties, were talking with Becka and her husband Charlie and their now eighteen-year-old son, Brock.

"Grandpa," Brock said, "I forgot to tell you, I got into George Mason University! I start in the fall."

"Well, just look at you! Congratulations! Wonderful! Nana and I couldn't be prouder of you."

Aevery reached over and shook Brock's hand.

Just then, Jessica's husband burst through the door.

"He's here, our baby is here!"

"How is Jess?" Aevery asked.

"She had a hard time, but she's fine now. Come on in!"

Everyone got up to go to Jessica's room. Then filed in, slowly and quietly, and found Jessica holding her baby boy. She was exhausted but smiling. As Candace sat down beside her, Jessica handed Sean the baby. Jake hugged Sean from behind. Aevery standing next to them, smiled. Edward smiled, too.

Sean was nearly overcome with joy. "Awww, how precious. He's so little, just like you were, Jess."

"Our first great," Aevery said. "He's a beautiful boy, Jess." He wiped a tear.

Sean came over and handed the baby to

Candace, who beamed as she accepted the baby into her arms, "Born on Nana and Grandpa's fiftieth anniversary," she murmured. "This is quite a gift! Thanks, Jess and Carl. You couldn't have planned it better if you tried."

Everyone chuckled.

"Is it still your anniversary?" Jessica asked. "How late is it?"

Carl looked at his watch. "Yep. It's a quarter to midnight right now."

Jessica looked at Aevery, "Granddad, Carl and I decided on a name."

"Oh?"

"Our boy's name is Aevery Gerald Thomas, after both of our grandfathers."

Everyone groaned with delight.

One Sunday a few weeks later, Aevery sat alone in the church after Mass. He had lit a special candle.

"Edward, this candle is to honor you. I want to thank you. If it weren't for your intervening on my behalf, I would've missed all the good stuff. Thanks, Mister. I mean, you did good."

Edward smiled, and patted Aevery on the back.

Chapter Fifteen

A Good Marine

It was a cold and drizzly Tuesday when Sean and Jake, now in their sixties, drove up to the family home and ran to the door, where Candace, now in her eighties, greeted them. The rest of the family were already in the living room, including Jessica and her three children and Becka, her children, and her small grandchildren.

The past ten years had taken their toll on Aevery. He suffered from COPD, and diabetes, so severely that Candace had finally called in the hospice team.

"He's not doing well, honey" she whispered to Sean. "You better go in and see him."

Sean and Jake crept into the den where Aevery, looking very old and fragile, was lying in his hospital bed, the oxygen cannula in his nose. His breath was labored.

As Sean walked up to his father's bedside and touched him lightly on the arm, Aevery's eyes slowly opened. "Hey, Dad. How you doin'?" Sean felt scared and cautious.

Edward and the spirit of Cpl. Larson were standing near the head of the bed, though of course no one could see them.

Aevery raised one frail hand and took Sean's hand. "I'm getting ready to go," he whispered. "I've got my sea bag packed."

"Dad, you're not going anywhere."
Candace shook her head and signaled from the other side of the bed for Sean not to contradict his father.

"I have to leave soon," Aevery managed to say. "Sorry, son. I know I've been gone a lot."

"Can't be helped, Dad. You're a Marine," Sean said, trying to swallow his emotions and blink back his tears. "I love you, Dad." He quickly wiped his face, as a tear streamed down, not wanting to show any weakness.

"I love you, too, you've been a good son," Aevery coughed a few times. "Except for that time you were twenty and had to speak at my funeral." He closed his eyes. "You better get it right this time, Mister."

Sean frowned and shook his head. *I spoke at his funeral?* Confused, he turned to his mother, who was now standing behind him, and whispered, "Oh My God, why is he so confused?"

"He's getting close to…to going. He's been talking to someone named Edward, too. And someone named Larson." She shrugged her shoulders.

"How long before he…?" Sean asked.

"He just said he's leaving soon. And when has your dad lied about leaving?"

Trying desperately to hold it together, Sean turned back to the bed, but his tears betrayed him and streamed down his cheeks. Jake tried to console his husband by gently rubbing his shoulders. But he was tearful too.

"Hey, now," Aevery said, his voice getting weaker and weaker. "Can't you see I'm trying to rest?" I've got a long hump ahead of me. Let's just say our good-byes now, in case I'm not here when you get back. Go on now. All of you, please let me rest."

Sean rubbed his father's hand for the last time. "Okay, Dad. I love you. Have a good—trip." He kissed him on the forehead.

Aevery responded to the tender kiss, "Okay, son. See ya, see ya later."

As Candace ushered them out of the room, Aevery closed his eyes.

That night, the den was crowded with Warrior Spirits from all throughout time, men who had come to get Aevery. Spirits of Native American and African warriors, some with huge headdresses spears and shields, pushed in to see Aevery and pay him respect. Spirits of medieval armor-clad knights clanked up to his bed. Standing in a circle around his bed, the warriors of time watched as Aevery slept peacefully, his breathing getting slower and slower.

At last, he expired.

When Aevery's spirit came out of his body, the first one to greet him was Edward. His spirit was young again, and he wore his familiar USMC dress blue deltas. Dozens of his brothers-in-arms were also there to greet him, including Cpl. Larson.

He hugged his Guardian Angel, "Edward, you old hound dog. Good to be able to see you again, old friend." Aevery turned and shook Cpl. Larson's hand and patted him on the back.\

Cpl. Larson's eyes twinkled as he said, "Gunny—you ready for the for-real version this time?"

"I'm ready this time."

They all walked off together.

This funeral of Aevery's was a huge affair. The church was completely full. Half of the mourners were family members, the other half, friends and acquaintances that Aevery and Candace had made during their long and successful marriage. Candace was surrounded by her children, grandchildren, and great grandchildren, although her sister Margaret, still well dressed, with diamonds still flashing, did not sit with the family. Even Tony and his wife, children, and grandchildren were present.

Sean got up and walked to the lectern. Aevery's casket was covered by a flag, and a portrait of an older Aevery had been placed on an easel with a huge wreath of red, white, and blue flowers.

Sean was not nervous as he adjusted the microphone. "Today we celebrate the amazing life of my wonderful father. He took great pride in his children, his grandchildren, and his great grandchildren." He straightened up and cleared his throat. "He seemed to know how to handle our quirks and problems with such wisdom and finesse. He really was remarkable. He loved unconditionally, wholeheartedly, and selflessly." He took a deep breath and continued, "My mother and father went through a lot in their sixty years together, and their marriage was a wonderful example to all of us. My father seemed to strive to make my mother happy on a daily basis. It was really something!" He cleared his throat. "In making my mother happy, my father made us all happy. He was truly an inspiring man. He gave his wisdom and knowledge at times when we all needed it most." He looked around at the entire audience. "After he retired from the U.S. Marine Corps, he became very active in Alcoholics Anonymous and helped a lot of veterans with PTSD. In his later years, he and my mother traveled and had good times together. He planned our family reunions. He made us all feel loved." Sean's voice finally cracked, "We will all miss him very much. He was a wonderful husband, father, grandfather, great-grandfather, son, brother, uncle…and…A Good Marine."

Epilogue

Once his funeral was over and he had been counseled again, accompanied as usual by Edward, Aevery was reunited with his family on the Shining Isle. He mussed the hair of his now grown son. He hugged his mother, and his Nana and his Grandpa.

In a heavenly bowling alley, he bowled with Uncle Richard, Edward, and Cpl. Larson. They all wore very stylish bowling attire, including fingerless gloves and shirts with their names embroidered on them. Edward's shirt had little angel wings over his name and a halo over the A. As each bowler made a strike, they all high-fived each other.

Aevery also got to spend a lot of quality time with his mother. He and Janice practiced Tai Chi on the beach at sunrise. They sat in the lotus position on big pillows in her lavish treehouse and meditated, incense burning in the background. They sat together in a field of daisies, talking and laughing, both with daisy crowns in their hair.

Edward appeared again in front of the Seven Spiritual Beings of the Karmic Council.

Magda stood up first. "Congratulations, Edward, on a job well done."

All Seven Beings of The Karmic Council

applauded him.

But Edward looked hesitant.

"What is it, Edward?" Magda asked, "Do you wish to speak?"

Edward nodded.

"You may speak," she said.

"I've been a Guardian Angel for most of my existence," he began.

"Yes?" she said, wondering what he was getting at.

Edward spoke slowly. "Well…I would like to request permission to incarnate. I would like to be human."

Magda looked surprised and turned to look at the other Councilwomen, who were all stunned. She looked back at Edward.

Aevery stood in the Apple Orchard with a huge crowd of family. A soft, perfumed breeze was blowing, and apple blossoms were drifting through the air. It was like a perfect spring day.

"Do I look okay?" he asked Janice.

"You look fine, dear," she answered as she straightened his tie.

Suddenly the crowd began buzzing with excitement.

Carol shouted, "Here they come!"

Candace appeared from a clearing in the forest, accompanied by Alice.

"There she is!" Aevery shouted. He ran to her;

she started to run, too. They embraced and kissed as he lifted her up, swinging her around. He set her back down and caressed her face. "Mrs. Warrier."

"Husband of mine."

"Welcome to the Isle of Apples. Come and meet our son."

The End

Resources for Veterans

Marine DESTRESS Line "Marine to Marine"
1-877-476-7734

Veteran Crisis Line
1-800-273-8255 - press 1
or text to 838255

stopveteransuicide.org

thegarysinisefoundation.org

Acknowledgments

I would like to thank my eldest son, Leverto Olmedo, who consulted with me extensively on the screenplay *A GOOD MARINE*, which I adapted into this novel. He helped me with Marine Corps jargon, how a Marine would react in the situations in which Aevery Warrier finds himself, Aevery's service record, uniforms and Marine Corps culture. He encouraged me every step of the way and congratulated me every time *A GOOD MARINE* placed in the screenplay competitions.

I want to thank Philippe Meade Design, Inc. for the artwork on the cover, and a special thanks to my Son, Loy Olmedo's company, Pure Signs Wholesale (www.puresignswholesale.com), especially Sam Arieta, for turning my movie poster into a book cover.

I want to thank my husband, Guy Thompson, for helping me to work out certain details of the Screenplay A GOOD MARINE, including Aevery's service record. The script would not be what it is today, nor the novel, without his help. He also helped me with the titles of the chapters and with formatting before publishing…especially the page numbering.

I want to thank my screenwriting mentor, Monica Lee Bellais, who encouraged me and taught me the importance of script formatting and industry standard, which helped me to become the storyteller

I am today. I want to thank Monica and Women in Film and Video DC for selecting *A GOOD MARINE* to be in the 2016 Spotlight On Screenwriters Catalogue.

I want to thank the Toronto International Screenwriting Competition for honoring *A GOOD MARINE* with third place in their 2018 competition.

I want to thank the Military Script Showcase for selecting *A GOOD MARINE* as an Official Selection in their end-of-2018 competition.

I want to thank the Filmmakers International Screenwriting Awards for recognizing *A GOOD MARINE* as a Quarterfinalist, Semifinalist, and Finalist for their 2018 competition.

A big thank you to my editor Barbara Ardinger, Ph.D. (www.barbaraardinger.com), whose talents with words seem to be endless. She is the reason this book reads like butter. Thank you also to Sue Jorgenson who proofread the manuscript before publishing. Thank you both for your talents and for the work you do to make literature more enjoyable.

I want to thank my brother-in-law, Gregory Payran Thompson, whose untimely suicide gave me the inspiration for this story, and his family, who allowed me to dedicate this book to him.

Thank you to my family, all of my children, friends, and co-workers who have been so encouraging of me in my writing career. Much love to you all.

About the Author

Tracey L. Thompson is a native of southern California and now resides in the Washington, D.C. area. Her debut novel Fatropolis was published in 2012. She adapted her book to a screenplay, and it was featured in the 2015 Spotlight on Screenwriters Catalogue. Her next screenplay, A GOOD MARINE was featured in the 2016 Catalogue, and a third work, UNTIL WE MEET AGAIN, was featured in the 2017 Catalogue. Now, A GOOD MARINE has placed in three different screenwriting competitions within one year.

As a young adult, she worked as a roofer, a janitor, and a Dairy Queen girl. During her first marriage to a native Mexican, she became fluent in Spanish, had four beautiful children (three boys and a girl) and lived in Mexico for a time. While overcoming domestic violence, divorce, and single motherhood, she started attending college, and worked as a barber on a Marine Corps base. She takes pride in having once done ninety haircuts in one day!

She eventually earned a master's degree in psychology with a specialization in marriage & family therapy. In the year 2000, she met and married her current husband, and five years later welcomed another son. It was then that she became interested in writing and storytelling. In the last eighteen years of her professional career, she has worked with victims of domestic violence, terminally ill patients, at-risk youth; has trained military families about resiliency; and now serves as a bilingual social worker at the county level assisting needy families and the homeless. She is also a trained interpreter for English and Spanish.

Now the grandmother of eight beautiful grandchildren, four girls and four boys. She searched for many years for a satisfying spiritual path as one of Jehovah's Witnesses and as a devout Catholic, but finally found her spiritual niche in the study of Shamanism, Feng Shui, and Reiki. Her interests include spending time with her family, writing, watching movies, drumming, making jewelry, knitting, scrapbooking, music, and playing Dungeons & Dragons.

Other Books

by

Tracey L. Thompson

FATROPOLIS A NOVEL – Jenny Crandell wants to be happy despite being overweight. When she prays for a miracle to find her Mr. Right, and then falls into a parallel world where fat bodies are the ideal, she gets to see what life is like for the beautiful people. This story is for anyone who has ever felt "less than." Especially for men and women who are overweight. Have you ever wondered where size and weight discrimination started? Fatropolis is that story.

Available in paperback and digital, from:

- Pearlsong Press – www.pearlsongpress.com
- www.amazon.com and Kindle
- Your favorite online bookstore

Currently In The Works

UNTIL WE MEET AGAIN - The Spirit of a teen who died in 1952 is approved to reincarnate, just as her elderly sister is diagnosed as terminally ill. When her contract to reincarnate gets cancelled, she must find a way to get it reinstated before another Soul "walks in" to the life that was destined for her. This story is for anyone who has lost a loved one. Many people are convinced of Life after Death, and this story explores that very concept. Going on after a loved one's death can be difficult, but if only we could see behind the scenes of what our loved ones are doing on the Other Side, it might comfort us, or even make us laugh.